ARTIFACTS OF DEATH

A MURDER MYSTERY IN UTAH'S CANYON COUNTRY

RICH CURTIN

Copyright © 2010, 2016 Rich Curtin
All rights reserved.

ISBN: 1453890858
ISBN-13: 9781453890851
Library of Congress Control Number: 2010915606

Printed in the United States of America

Dedicated to the Memory of
Tony Hillerman

PROLOGUE

Southeast Utah
September 4ᵗʰ 1938

LIAM SLOWLY PUSHED aside a branch of the juniper tree that concealed him and peered down Burro Canyon in the direction from which he'd just hiked. He was nearly sick from worrying. His great fear was that someone would follow him to the cave. No one but Liam knew of its existence or the valuable treasures it contained. It was just above him, a hundred feet up the rocky talus slope to the canyon wall, and behind the boulder that concealed its opening. As he waited and watched, he fought back a nagging fear, a fear that he was in way over his head. He was just a simple ranch hand engaged in what seemed to be an overly complicated endeavor. But if he did everything just right, he would soon be a rich man.

He lingered for a few minutes just to be certain. Then, seeing no one, he emerged from behind the juniper and scampered to the top of the talus. He took

1

one final glance up and down the canyon to make sure he was alone. Then he squeezed his lanky frame through the small opening behind the boulder and entered Josh's private cave.

Inside, he paused and allowed his eyes to adjust to the darkness. All was quiet. The air was stale and musty but its coolness against his sweaty skin was a welcome relief from the heat in the canyon. He struck a wooden match on the rock wall, located Josh's kerosene lantern, and ignited it. He found a clear place on the floor and sat down, placing the lantern on top of a nearby rock.

As the flame grew and the cave brightened, Liam could see the dozens of Indian pots, bowls, and plates his friend Josh had stored there over the years. Ancient ceramic treasures from the Anasazi, Fremont, and Mogollon peoples, as well as more recent works of art from various Pueblo tribes. Strange-looking figurines of Mayan origin were interspersed among the other artifacts.

Liam reached out and picked up an eight-hundred-year-old Anasazi bowl, cradled it in his calloused hands, and stared at it, wondering what it was worth. He was surprised at how little it weighed. As he gently returned it to its resting place, the enormity of the problem facing him began to sink in. How could he convert all the pots into cash without tipping his hand? First of all, the cave was on private property. It was located in a remote area on the back end of the Rutherford Ranch, up

Cottonwood Canyon and into a tributary called Burro Canyon. Josh had told him that ranch personnel rarely came up here because the grazing was so poor, but one still had to be on the lookout. Certainly, coming in here in a vehicle or on horseback was out of the question. That meant transporting the pots two or three at a time in a backpack. He would have to leave his horse on the public lands on top of the mesa and hike the three miles down to the cave and back. Secondly, when he returned to Moab with the pots, he would have to keep them concealed and sell them in secrecy. Maybe he could entrust Billy McKnight, his friend in Monticello who was a part-time artifact dealer. But so many trips to the cave would be required. How could he pull it off without people becoming suspicious and following him back to the cave?

Liam surveyed his surroundings. The ceramic treasures were everywhere, the large ones on the floor along the walls of the cave, the smaller ones in natural nooks and recesses up higher. Josh had placed each one on a protective bed of straw. As Liam's eyes surveyed the collection, his appreciation of his deceased friend grew. The artifacts were worth a small fortune, especially by Liam's ranch-hand standards. And now they were his.

This sudden wealth meant he and Becky would now have enough money to marry and begin their life together. He removed the tobacco pouch from his shirt pocket, rolled a cigarette, and lit it from the lamp. He loved Becky with all his heart, but his pride hadn't allowed him to set a date for their wedding until he was able to provide her with a proper home. So they were both saving every penny they could. But now everything was about to change. He pushed back his sweat-stained cowboy hat, slid her picture out of his wallet, and looked at it in the flickering light. Becky smiled at him. She was 24 years old, pretty, with fair skin, light brown hair, and hazel eyes. Liam knew he was a lucky man. He couldn't understand exactly what she saw in an uneducated, raw-boned, thirty-year-old ranch hand with hair like straw, but he was grateful.

Then the cold realization that Josh was gone forever entered his thoughts as it often did, and transformed his mood into one of melancholy. His best friend, mentor, and father figure had been known as a world-class trader for decades throughout the Four Corners area. He missed him.

Liam grunted as he stood up, his leg muscles stiff from the long hike. He picked up the lantern, held it out in front of him, and began a close inspection of the cave's contents. Taking small steps, he moved around the dark interior, conscious of the possibility of cracking his head on a rock jutting out from the dark, and equally conscious of the need to avoid stepping on the fragile pottery. He reflected on Josh and the many trips he must have made to this place, each trip adding another valuable item to the collection. He could almost see his friend standing there, a pot resting in his large hands, scanning the cave in the flickering light, deciding where to place it. Every piece had its own story, and he wished his friend were still alive so he could ask him about each one, how he'd gotten it, and what he'd traded for it. Sadly, Josh had taken his life with his favorite pistol rather than let the pain of the spreading cancer rob him of his dignity.

But, Liam considered, at 78 years of age, the large, loud, happy-go-lucky Josh had had a full life. The Santa look-alike had come west in 1878 and helped settle the Four Corners area. For six decades, Josh had traveled in a horse-drawn wagon, and later in an old Ford truck, across Utah, Arizona, New Mexico, and Colorado, bringing needed supplies to settlers in remote areas. He'd been famous for trading merchandise, spreading know-how, and telling tall tales, and everyone wanted to be his friend. Few men ever had a better life, Liam finally decided.

He took another drag on his cigarette, and recalled the time his friend had taken him to the cave and told him to memorize the route. Josh must have suspected then that the cancer was terminal. Then, a few months later while Liam was visiting his bedridden friend, Josh reached over and grasped his arm. The once strong grip felt soft and weak. Josh had spoken in a whisper, "Liam, you're my best friend in the whole world. I'll be departing this beautiful earth real soon. I'm leaving all the pottery in the cave to you. Keep it real secret. It'll fetch a good sum of money. Now hurry up and marry that pretty girl of yours." A few days later, Josh was dead by his own hand.

The memory of all this kept swirling in Liam's mind as he studied the contents of the cave. To a simple ranch hand, the whole situation was a bit overwhelming. His thoughts reverted to Becky. In his most recent letters, he'd told her about the trip to Josh's cave, the remarkable treasures it contained, and the sad passing of his best friend. He had another letter in his shirt pocket to mail to her as soon as he got back to Moab. He grinned as he imagined Becky reading it. She would be beaming. It said he would be coming to Colorado Springs at the end of the month and since he was now financially secure they could marry right away. He thought he could sell about a dozen pieces of pottery by then. Finally, they'd be able to buy that small ranch they had often talked about. They could begin a life together.

Liam had purchased a small silver locket from a Navajo silversmith in Moab. It was heart-shaped and inlaid with tiny turquoise, coral, and obsidian stones. It opened by pressing a catch on the side. Liam had cut his and Becky's smiling faces from a small photograph and pressed them into opposite sides of the locket. Wrapped in cotton cloth, the locket was in the envelope along with his letter. His message ended with the words, "All my love always, Liam."

Liam took a final drag from his cigarette and crushed the butt under his boot. As he progressed toward the rear of the cave, something higher up in the far wall caught his eye. Holding the lantern high, he could see three figurines residing in a nook side by side. They were adorned with red, white, and yellow designs. Each was about twelve inches high, with outstretched arms, and faces that seemed to look with surprise at this cowboy intruder. Intrigued, he decided to take one down for a closer look. He placed the lantern on the floor and stepped up onto a narrow ledge about two feet high that Josh must have stood on when he put them there. As his face got closer to the figurines and he could see them more clearly, he became fascinated by their bizarre expressions. Standing on his tip-toes, he reached for the one with the wide open eyes and oval-shaped mouth, grasping it with both hands.

At that instant, Liam felt a sharp pain in his left wrist, even before the snake's telltale rattle fully registered in his mind. He jerked his hand back in fear, lost his balance, and fell backwards to the floor of the cave, striking his head sharply on the edge of a rock. While he lay there unconscious, the venom proceeded to do its work. Liam and his dreams passed that afternoon into the next world.

1

FROM HIS VANTAGE point behind a fallen slab of sandstone, Frank Sorenson trained his Swarovski binoculars down Cottonwood Canyon. He scanned from the immediate foreground to a point a quarter-mile distant where a bend in the canyon blocked further view. He repeated the process several times, inspecting each rock, juniper, and shadow. There could be no mistakes. None. Too much at stake. And there was no rush, he had plenty of time. He would go to the cave, wrap three of the Ancient Indian pots in bubble-wrap, and place them in his specially constructed backpack. Then he would hike back up the canyon to the mesa top, traverse the two miles to his pickup truck, and drive out on the gravel roads of the LaSal Mountains. Just as he'd done five times before. He knew exactly which three pots he would take out on this trip, and how much cash he would get for each. The total this time would be $32,500 tax-free dollars.

Suddenly he froze, thinking he saw movement farther down in the canyon. He readjusted the focus of the binoculars and concentrated on the spot where he thought he'd seen motion. Nothing moved. He stared until tears began to well up in his eyes. Looking away, he blinked until he regained clear vision, and then resumed his surveillance. If necessary, he would abort this trip to the cave and come back another day.

As a former sniper in the U.S. Army Special Forces, Sorenson had always taken great pride in the meticulous planning and patient execution of his missions. He'd made a practice of analyzing each step in his plan for things that could go wrong, and thinking through a contingency plan for each potential problem. Quick decisions, no missteps, no undue risks. In his plan to empty the cave of its artifact treasures and sell them for a large profit, he'd resurrected his Army instincts and was now putting them into practice. At 58 years of age, he felt in fairly good shape. But not like his days in the Army. Now, when he looked at himself in the mirror, he still saw the same square jaw and piercing blue eyes, but his stocky frame had become six inches larger around the waist and his once dark-brown buzz cut had turned mostly gray.

He was considering a retreat. Then he noticed movement again behind a stand of junipers farther down the canyon. Two cows, each with a calf, slowly emerged from behind the trees on their quest for fresh grass. He relaxed. He decided to watch another half-hour before proceeding, just to be sure. He'd been spotted in the lower part of Cottonwood Canyon once before. It was during his initial search for the cave. A young Hispanic ranch hand had informed him in no uncertain terms that he was on private land, that the lower part of the canyon was on the Rutherford Ranch, and that it was posted. Sorenson apologized for his error, saying he was a hiker and thought he was still on Bureau of Land Management property. The ranch hand considered that for a moment, forced a thin smile, and pointed out that the BLM land ended at the cattle guard with the no-trespassing signs. Embarrassed and humiliated, Sorenson retreated back up the rocky two-track road that wound its way up Cottonwood Canyon. The ranch hand just waited there and watched him the whole way. He was sure his cover story had been believable, but vowed never to make that mistake again. He couldn't afford to be seen a second time on the privately-owned land, and certainly not by the same ranch hand. Waiting another thirty minutes before resuming his mission was a sensible precaution.

He found a shady spot near the wall of the canyon and sat down. Glancing at his watch, he made a mental note of the time. He leaned back against a block of sandstone, removed his faded green cap, and relaxed.

His schedule allowed for such contingencies so the delay wouldn't be a problem. He looked out at the immense red rock walls that enclosed him. The narrow band of blue sky visible at the top of the canyon was populated with large cumulus clouds made bright white by the rising sun. It was a crisp, early-October morning and cool air descended from the LaSal Mountains, bringing with it the fresh scent of sagebrush.

This was his sixth trip down the canyon to retrieve some of the treasure, each previous visit having been exceedingly profitable. A slight smile moved his lips as he pictured the cave and its valuable contents. Most of the artifacts were museum-quality pieces. And he had no trouble selling them. He was accumulating wealth and with it came an unfamiliar feeling of success and stature. But it was the discovery of the cave in the first place that made him proud of himself in many ways. It was brilliant work actually, and when all this was over, with the cave empty and the contents sold, he would enjoy recounting the story to the people with whom he associated.

Thirty minutes later, he rose up on one knee, peered through his binoculars, and inspected the trail ahead. Seeing nothing out of the ordinary, he resumed his hike down the canyon. He stopped each quarter-mile, looking and listening for any sign of another human. By now the route was familiar to him. He'd grown accustomed to the sound of the breeze rustling the rabbit brush, the occasional trill of a canyon wren, and the contrast of the red sandstone cliffs against the dark blue sky. After three hours of slow, cautious hiking, he reached the mouth of Burro Canyon and turned right. He proceeded up-canyon a short distance, stopped, and removed his backpack. He pulled a plastic water bottle from one of the side pockets and took a drink. Then he placed the backpack out of sight behind a rock, wiped his forehead with his sleeve, and took one last look around.

Sorenson was keenly aware that this was the most critical part of the operation. He couldn't chance anyone seeing him enter or leave the cave. He had to work fast. He had pre-sold the three particular pots he would retrieve on this trip. The buyer was an Indian artifact dealer in Farmington, New Mexico. They had agreed on the prices based on photographs he had taken during an earlier visit to the cave. He removed a pair of work gloves from his back pocket, put them on, and got busy.

He walked up the side canyon a dozen yards from where he'd left the backpack and then clambered up the talus slope toward the canyon wall. The talus rose up about one hundred feet from the canyon floor and consisted of rocks of all sizes which had fallen off the cliff face over the millennia. Rabbit brush, junipers, and snakeweed had sprouted and grown here and there on the talus, rooting wherever windblown soil had accumulated in the spaces between the rocks. A small cluster of medium-sized junipers grew directly in front of the narrow opening to the cave, helping to shield it from the view of a passerby on the canyon floor. He reached the cave, pushed aside the juniper branches, and squeezed himself through an opening behind the large slab of fallen cap rock which concealed the entrance.

He ignited the propane lantern he'd left there, located the first pot, and picked it up with both hands. It was a St. John's polychrome about ten inches across, and in perfect condition. A real beauty. He exited the cave, holding the piece out in front of him with care, allowing it to rest in his open palms. He was well aware that the pots were fragile due to the micro-cracking which aging inevitably produced. A slight mishandling or a misstep on the talus could prove to be expensive. He again scanned the canyon. All clear. Taking short steps, he descended the slope, testing each rock to ensure it was stable before putting his full weight on it. Once on the canyon floor, he walked back to the rock which concealed his backpack and placed the pot on the flat sandy ground in front of it. He made a second trip to the cave, obtained a seven inch black-on-white Mimbres pot, carried it back, and gently placed it in the sand near the first pot. He returned to the cave and retrieved the third item, a small grey Fremont pot with a white sawtooth design around its circumference.

Turning off the lantern as he exited the cave, he descended the talus and walked toward the other two pots. Almost finished, he thought. Easy money.

It was then that he saw the ranch hand striding toward him. Startled, he stopped in his tracks.

"Hey! What are you doing here? This is private . . . Oh, it's you again!" It was the same ranch hand who had spotted him on his first foray into Burro Canyon.

"I thought I told you not to . . . Hey, what are those?" the ranch hand said, pointing to the two pots on the ground as he approached them wide-eyed with curiosity. He bent over to get a closer look. Sorenson fired a nine-millimeter slug into the top of his head. Dead instantly, the ranch hand fell forward, directly on top of the Mimbres pot, shattering it into dozens of pieces, even as echoes of the gunshot returned from the cliff faces.

"Damn," said Sorenson out loud. He'd realized too late that he should have made the guy back away from the pots before killing him. In his planning process, he had considered the problem of an intruder and what he would do about it. But he hadn't foreseen the possibility of a broken pot.

Scanning the area and seeing no one else, he slipped his Glock 17 back into the holster under his shirt and got to work. From the backpack, he removed sheets of bubble-wrap and a roll of masking tape. He wrapped the polychrome pot and placed it into one of three padded compartments in his backpack. He repeated the process with the Fremont pot, placing it in the next space. Then he rolled the dead ranch hand over onto his back and collected the pieces of the broken pot. He placed them in several Ziploc bags and wrapped each bag in bubble-wrap. Glancing about as he worked, he was relieved to see no one. He placed the bags of potsherds into the third compartment. He was irritated he'd lost part of his prize money, but knew the sherds could be cemented back into a whole pot that would still have significant value. Before leaving, he picked up a few pieces of dried-out rabbit brush and swept out his tracks back to the talus.

With great care, he lifted the backpack into place on his shoulders, slid his arms through the straps and fastened the harness clips. Driven by adrenaline, he strode out of Burro Canyon and back up Cottonwood Canyon to the mesa top, not stopping to rest. He headed toward his vehicle, a 1997 red Toyota Tacoma pickup which he'd left hidden in the junipers just off the Thompson Canyon Trail. While he was hiking, his logical mind reviewed the situation. The ranch hand would be missed and sooner or later someone would come looking for him. When the body was discovered, Cottonwood Canyon and Burro Canyon would be crawling with law enforcement personnel. He was fairly certain no one would find the cave during the investigation as it was well above the canyon floor. The entrance was virtually impossible to see from below, even if you knew exactly where to look. And if the authorities decided to inspect along the narrow terraces on top of the talus, they would still be unlikely to discover the opening because of the junipers which hid it. It was clear he would have to exercise extreme caution on subsequent trips to the cave. He'd wait a few days before resuming his visits.

Sorenson removed his backpack, wrapped it in foam padding, and placed it on the passenger-side floor of his truck. He started the engine and began his journey out of the LaSal Mountains. As he carefully drove the gravel roads, he reflected on what he'd done. In the past, killing a man had never bothered him. He had killed nearly two dozen as a sniper in Viet Nam and Cambodia. But this was different. In the Army, he'd killed at a distance and then retreated back into the jungle. This time, he saw the bloody result lying right in front of him. It produced an entirely different feeling. Very upsetting and very personal. He began to feel queasy. He'd always been terrified of corpses anyway, regardless of the cause of death. And he dreaded having to go near that desiccated skeleton in the rear of the cave, although he certainly did so whenever necessary to retrieve the pots and figurines stored back there.

He'd always believed his fear of corpses was a result of finding that dead nun when he was in the fifth grade at St. Joseph's Catholic School in Cleveland. A good student and an altar boy, he'd been selected by the nuns to go at noon from the school to the convent two blocks away. His job was to pick up the hot lunch prepared in the kitchen and carry it back to the teachers' lounge. He enjoyed the special feeling that came with this prestigious appointment. And there was a side benefit: he was excused from class fifteen minutes early. One day he arrived at the kitchen and instead of finding the food, he found the cook, Sister Mary Carmen, dead on the floor. He looked at her grey-green face and froze. He tried to cry out for help but couldn't. And for some reason he couldn't turn away. Fifteen minutes later they'd found him there, trembling over the corpse. He'd been taken to a local hospital and treated for shock, but forever after he'd had a chilling fear of corpses.

As he drove, Sorenson tried to stay calm and analyze the consequences of his actions. But his stomach was upset and his face was breaking out in a cold sweat. The realization of what he'd done was sinking in. Having a plan to shoot an intruder that caught him red-handed was one thing. Kind of clean and antiseptic. But actually *doing* it was something else entirely. And even though he no longer believed in an afterlife, his Catholic value system was deeply ingrained in his psyche. It began to dawn on him that unlike his sniper activities in the Army, this was *murder*. He became acutely nauseous, stopped the truck, got out, and threw up.

After a few minutes' rest and a drink of water, the clammy feeling faded. He hoisted himself back into his vehicle, pulled the door closed, and resumed driving. An hour later, he reached the south side of the mountains, left the gravel of Two Mile Road behind, and turned onto the pavement of Highway 46. He struggled to refocus his thoughts. Three things required immediate attention. First and foremost, he would wipe the gun clean including the magazine and bullets, then dispose of them where they would never be found. He'd made a practice of wiping down the bullets before loading them into the magazine, but he would repeat the process as a further precaution. He'd bought the Glock at a gun show in Tucson ten years ago. It had never been registered in his name. Still, he had to be careful. He would take a detour tomorrow to Lake Powell, cross the lake on the small ferry at Hall's Crossing, and dump the works overboard.

The second thing to do was get rid of his shirt and pants. It was possible someone had spotted him leaving the canyon and would provide a description to the authorities. Also, some of the dead ranch hand's blood might have spattered onto his clothing. Come to think of it, he would get rid of the boots as well. There was always the chance an investigator might match them to the boot prints in the canyon. The faded green cap he would keep. It was his favorite and just too hard to part with. He had extra clothing and an old pair of hiking boots in the storage unit he rented in Blanding. He would change clothes there before going to his motel room. In the morning he would go to the Blanding public dump and dispose of the clothing and boots.

That decided, he moved to the third item. He would have to contact the artifact dealer in Farmington and tell him there would be only two pots instead of the promised three. The deal would have to be re-priced. This change in plan irritated Sorenson since he'd been so careful to arrange the whole operation such that the dealer never knew his identity. And he wanted to keep it that way. If the dealer ever learned who his supplier was, it would be a simple matter to tail Sorenson and discover the location of the cave. He had even taken the precaution of always wearing gloves when handling the artifacts so he couldn't be traced by his fingerprints. He disliked any deviation from the standard procedure where the dealer was involved. Deviations invited mistakes. Oh well, he thought, one long-distance phone call from a pay phone should take care of the problem. His anonymity would remain intact.

It was evening by the time he reached Blanding. He drove to his storage unit, left the pots and the backpack there, and changed his clothes. Using a public telephone outside a convenience store, he made the call to Farmington and renegotiated the deal. He proceeded to the motel, checked in using an alias, and paid in cash. So far, so good. Tomorrow morning, he would drive to the dump and then to the lake.

That night, as he sat in his room, he told himself that after the whole operation was completed, he would compartmentalize in his mind the evil deed he'd done, seal it off, and forget it. Then he'd be able to return to a normal life consistent with his Catholic value system.

2

HAVING JUST FINISHED lunch, Paul Williamson got up from the kitchen table, kissed his wife Sarah on the cheek, and stepped outside onto the large covered porch which wrapped around the sprawling ranch house. The house, constructed of massive spruce logs, served as headquarters for the Rutherford Ranch, a cattle operation with land on both sides of the Dolores River. He stretched, pushed back his cowboy hat, and looked upward. He saw a few scattered cumulus clouds in an otherwise blue sky, but no sign of the thunderstorms the weatherman had promised.

As ranch foreman, he could control just about everything at the ranch except the weather—and the cracks appearing in the pastures meant rain was needed soon. He hoped the forecast was right this time. Williamson, a tall broad-shouldered man in his early 50s, glanced over at the old man in the rocking chair. His slow oscillations made the floorboards of the porch creak, the only sounds in an otherwise quiet afternoon. As he did each day, the old man sat stiffly while he rocked, staring out toward the Dolores River in the distance.

"Howdy," said Williamson. He received no response, nor did he expect one. The old man, in his mid-eighties, was hard of hearing, seldom spoke, and exhibited early signs of dementia. He simply continued his incessant rocking and staring.

Eddie Stokes, Williamson's top hand, ambled toward the porch from the equipment maintenance shed. Passing in front of the old man, he bowed his head slightly and said, "Good afternoon, Mr. Rutherford." Again, no response, no reaction. Stokes stopped in front of the porch steps and looked up at Williamson. "Paul, when you're in Cortez tomorrow, we need some more air and fuel filters."

"OK Eddie. Give me a list and I'll pick everything up after the cattle auction. Right now, I'm going to ride out and help with that re-fencing on the south end of the ranch."

Williamson descended the steps and headed toward the corral to saddle up his horse. As he did, it crossed his mind that the part of the job he loved most was being in the saddle and working with his ranch hands. He disliked office work intensely, but Sarah, having a Bachelor's degree in accounting, took care of most of the paperwork. He remembered that day eighteen years ago, with the operations of the Rutherford Ranch faltering due to mismanagement and a prolonged period of below-average rainfall, when Mr. Rutherford had hired him as ranch foreman to turn things around. And turn things around he did. He took great pride in the fact that, during the ensuing years, the pastures had been restored, fences and buildings repaired, the herd upgraded to registered Herefords and tripled in size, and a profitable peach orchard planted adjacent to the Dolores River. Even the old ranch house had received a facelift.

He knew he was regarded not only as a competent rancher but also a fair-minded employer and a good neighbor. His success had brought offers of employment from larger ranches in Colorado and Utah, usually for substantially more money, but he and Sarah loved their life on the Rutherford Ranch. They had developed a close circle of friends in the Moab area. Also, Sarah had worked for many years as a volunteer supporting the Moab Home for Needy Children and now served as its Board Chairwoman. She had become very attached to the home and its young residents and could never leave them. So he and Sarah had remained at the Rutherford Ranch and made it their home. But with the success of the ranch came a burdensome amount of paperwork. Herd genetics, payroll, taxes, revenues, expenses, equipment maintenance schedules, and a host of other items had to be tracked and analyzed. As he saddled his horse, Williamson thought about how fortunate he was that Sarah handled the office chores, leaving him more time to work outdoors. His love and appreciation of Sarah were strong. And the work she did at the children's home made him proud. He would do anything to protect her happiness.

As he mounted his pinto, he noticed in the distance a saddled horse without a rider loping back in from the west pastures.

"Hey Eddie, whose horse is that?"

Eddie raised his hand to shade his eyes from the sun. "Looks like Jesse Montoya's mount. He went out early this morning into Cottonwood Canyon looking for those strays. I'd better go check on him. He's still a little green, but I never expected he'd lose his horse." Both men chuckled.

"Never mind, Eddie, I'll go myself," said Williamson. He considered the possibilities for a moment. "I'd better take the truck in case he got himself injured." He dismounted, handed the reins to Eddie, and got into his Dodge 4X4 pickup truck. He drove west on a two-track ranch road, slowing down as he transitioned to the rough road leading up Cottonwood Canyon. He hoped Montoya wasn't injured, but if he was, there was a first-aid kit in the glove compartment and Williamson had experience in treating wounds common to ranch work.

Montoya occupied Williamson's thoughts as he negotiated the challenging canyon road. He had been working at the ranch only four months. He was quiet and pretty much kept to himself. Since he was from South Texas and new to this area, not much was known about him. Where Montoya went during his days off from the ranch was anyone's guess, but the other ranch hands said he reeked of marijuana smoke when he returned. But Montoya was a hard worker and didn't make trouble. Williamson grinned as he imagined Montoya's horse just walking off and leaving him out there in the canyon. If that's what happened, he was in store for some serious ribbing from the boys.

As the truck lurched up the canyon in low gear, Williamson maneuvered over and around the rocks, all the while keeping his eyes open for Montoya. He noticed dark rain clouds accumulating west of the LaSal Mountains and hoped they would move east toward the ranch. Could be the weather man was right.

After nearly an hour of bone-jarring driving and intermittent stops to inspect the ground for hoof prints, he reached the point where Burro Canyon entered Cottonwood Canyon from his left. He stopped the truck to take a look up Burro Canyon and spotted a Levi-clad man lying on the ground a short distance away. Grabbing the first-aid kit, he jumped out of the truck and trotted over. Montoya was on his back, eyes closed. Williamson felt for a pulse and found none. Alarmed, he probed again. Nothing. Then he noticed the bloody hair on Montoya's head. His immediate thought was that the young ranch hand had been thrown from his horse and hit his head on a rock. But after a closer inspection, he saw the bullet hole. His first reaction was one of self-preservation. Thinking someone had shot Montoya from atop the canyon walls, he crouched and backpedaled to the truck, scanning the cliff-tops for any sign of a threat. He grabbed his 30-06 rifle from the gun rack and knelt behind his truck, inspecting both canyons and the top edges of the canyon walls. He saw no one. After a time, he walked back over to the body, and knelt down on one knee. Poor kid. Maybe he got himself mixed up in some kind of drug trouble. Maybe he was dealing. Williamson felt a sense of regret, even guilt, thinking he should have taken the marijuana reports more seriously and counseled Montoya. Or fired him.

Williamson stood up and scanned the area again. He took off his hat, wiped his forehead with his sleeve, and stood there, considering the situation. Montoya was dead. There was nothing he could do for the young man now. He walked back to his truck, reached through the open window and grabbed the radio's handset, intending to call the authorities. Then he stopped. Reconsidered. He returned the handset to its cradle and thought about the inevitable investigation the sheriff's office would conduct. There would be a lot of questions about Montoya and his drug use, and whether or not he was dealing. There would also be a lot of questions about the ranch itself. A probing of the Rutherford Ranch's operations was something he couldn't risk. The stakes were too high.

He returned the rifle to the gun rack and walked back to the body. He bent over and picked it up, holding one of Montoya's arms around his neck to support the weight. He put his other arm around Montoya's waist and carried him back to the truck, the dead ranch hand's feet dragging in the sand of the canyon floor. Williamson placed the body in the passenger-side seat and closed the door. He retrieved Montoya's hat, returned to his pickup, took one last look around, and pulled himself into the truck.

Williamson drove up Cottonwood Canyon, crossed over the cattle guard, and exited the ranch. Now on BLM land, he bounced two miles up the rocky canyon road to the Kokopelli Trail crossing at the edge of Fisher Valley. He would leave the body there. The trail was popular with mountain bikers and hikers, and he was sure someone would find Montoya soon and call the authorities.

He stopped the truck, got out, and looked around. No one else was in the area. He removed Montoya's body from the truck and gently placed it by the side of the trail. He tossed his hat nearby. A rumble of thunder made him look up. Towering thunderheads were moving his way and the landscape was darkening in shadow. He could smell the rain and feel the temperature dropping as the wind ushered in cooler air. Lightening flashed and the thunderclaps grew louder.

He jumped into his truck, wheeled it around, and started back down Cottonwood Canyon toward the ranch. He realized that moving Montoya's body was probably a serious crime, but it needed to be done. What was going on at the ranch had to be kept secret, whatever the risk. The life he and Sarah shared depended on it. As he drove, he examined the probable questions he would receive from the authorities, finally deciding that the questioning would be routine. The sheriff would conclude, as he himself did, that the killing was drug related. Anxious but relatively satisfied, he tried to force his thoughts to less unpleasant matters, like the coming of the rain and the cattle auction he would be attending in Cortez for the next two days. As he exited the bumpy road of the canyon and drove on the smoother two-track road across the west pastures, the first raindrops began pelting his windshield. They were large and cold. He turned on the wipers, rolled up the window, and headed back toward the ranch house.

3

THE DAY STARTED simply enough for Grand County Deputy Sheriff Manny Rivera. His clock radio came to life at 6:00 A.M. with the sounds of KCYN, "Moab's Canyon Country Radio," transmitting from high in the LaSal Mountains. Willie Nelson was singing *My Heroes Have Always Been Cowboys* as Rivera rolled out of bed, rubbed his eyes, and ambled over to the window. He pushed aside the curtains and peered outside. The thunderstorms of yesterday evening had moved on and the sky was now clear. He smiled. Another beautiful day in Moab.

He showered, shaved, splashed on some Old Spice aftershave, and put on his tan, deputy sheriff's uniform. He stood in front of the mirror and ran a comb through his wavy dark brown hair. Manuel "Manny" Rivera was 31-years old, five-foot eleven, and had a friendly, confident face. His fellow deputies often told him he was considered by the ladies in town to be quite handsome. He wasn't so sure about that.

As he did each morning before heading out the door, he looked at the fish in the ten-gallon aquarium on his kitchen countertop. The resident guppies had multi-colored bodies and long graceful tails. They were in continuous motion in the corner of the tank closest to Rivera, wiggling in anticipation of the breakfast he was about to dispense. He dropped a pinch of tropical fish food into the tank and watched them eat.

Then it was his turn. The growling sounds emanating from his stomach reminded him it was time for sausage, eggs, toast, and coffee at the Rim Rock Diner. Especially coffee. He always looked forward to that first cup in the morning.

He exited the older two-bedroom house he rented near the center of town and walked to the white Ford F-150 four-wheel-drive pickup in the driveway. The air smelled fresh and clean. The top of the 1000-foot high Moab Rim, the soaring red rock escarpment that loomed over the town, was glowing a bright copper color as the rising sun began to illuminate it. He stopped for a moment and gazed at it. Magnificent. His vehicle, on the other hand was another matter. The Grand County Sheriff's Department insignia on the door was barely visible through the reddish-brown mud splattered all over the truck. He made a mental note to run it through the carwash after breakfast. Routine off-road patrolling during yesterday afternoon's sudden downpour had been the culprit.

He was thinking about the day ahead as he slid into his vehicle, backed out of the driveway, and proceeded toward Main Street. Most of Moab was still asleep, but the streets would soon be teeming with young men and women heading out to the surrounding canyons, mesas, and mountains in their four-wheel-drives in search of adventure. Many would be hauling ATVs or mountain bikes. Some would be transporting kayaks or rubber rafts to the Colorado River. Each year, during spring and fall when the weather was near-perfect, the population of Moab swelled from six thousand to over ten thousand as the tourists arrived. Besides Arches National Park, Canyonlands National Park, the Colorado River, and the LaSal Mountains, there were thousands of square miles of BLM land on which they could play. It was just a matter of time before Rivera and his fellow deputies would be called upon to assist in a search-and-rescue operation in the back-country. Inevitably, some inexperienced adventure seeker would get into a life-threatening situation and need help.

But the area was not always like this. Rivera had learned from the old uranium prospectors who congregated each morning at the Rim Rock Diner that Moab was once a mining boomtown. Fifty years ago, demand for uranium was high as the world entered the nuclear age. But in the 1980s, the production of nuclear warheads and the construction of nuclear power plants in the U.S. had come to an end. The mines eventually closed and Moab fell on hard times. A typical boom and bust cycle according to the old prospectors.

As the mining activities faded into history, adventure tourism rose up to fill the economic void. Moab was reborn and resumed its growth. Restaurants, shops, and outfitters filled the old buildings. By day, tourists fanned out into the backcountry surrounding Moab, and by night they filled the restaurants, watering holes, and shops. Shorts and T-shirts were the uniform of the day. Rivera wondered what today would bring.

As he did on most workdays, he would meet his friend Emmett Mitchell for breakfast and banter. Mitchell was a deputy sheriff from San Juan County, the county just south of Grand County. The two were entertained each morning by the not-so-subtle flirtations and humorous coquetry of the diner's waitresses, particularly Betty, who was divorced four or five times and well into her 50s. A typical and enjoyable start to the workday for the men in uniform.

But this morning it was not to be. His cell phone rang and he fumbled to get it out of his pants pocket. He looked at the caller ID. It was Millie Ives, the sheriff's dispatcher. Since many Moab civilians had police scanners, sensitive conversations by the law enforcement community were conducted via cell phone.

"Manny, it's Millie. What's your location?"

Rivera detected a sense of urgency in her voice. "Good morning, Millie. I'm in town, on my way to the diner."

"Sheriff wants you to proceed immediately out to where the Kokopelli Trail crosses Cottonwood Canyon, out east of Fisher Valley. Three mountain bikers discovered a body there this morning. Young, male. They said it looked like he'd been shot in the head."

"Roger, Millie, I'm on my way." He made a quick U-turn on Main Street. "I guess it's granola bars for breakfast this morning."

"Manny, BLM and the Medical Examiner have been advised and are en route to the scene. The bikers called 9-1-1 from a cell phone to report the find. The operator asked them to remain at the scene until the authorities arrive."

"OK Millie. I figure it'll take me at least an hour to get out there. That area is remote and the runoff from yesterday's thunderstorms will make driving those back roads a slow go." He paused a moment and added, "Millie, will you call Emmett at the diner and tell him he won't have the pleasure of my company this morning?"

"Roger, Manny. Will do," she said. "Sorry about breakfast."

Rivera, thankful he had filled his fuel tank yesterday evening, drove north out of Moab, turned right on

Highway 128 and followed it northeast alongside the Colorado River. He reached down into the door pocket of his vehicle and extracted two granola bars from the supply he kept there for situations like this. Tearing open the first one with his teeth, he ate it, and washed it down with water from a plastic Aquafina bottle he periodically refilled from his kitchen tap. He repeated the process with the second granola bar.

Then he began considering the matter at hand. A homicide in the backcountry was unheard of in Grand County. The young people who ventured here for hiking, camping, or off-road driving were mostly law-abiding and clean-cut citizens. They were here to enjoy the great outdoors and each other. There were some who broke the rules and got into trouble. But generally the infractions were minor. Misdemeanors which could be attributed to the bad judgment of adolescence. But a *homicide*? He'd never heard of such a thing happening in these parts.

With his light bar silently flashing, he sped through the curves of Highway 128 as fast as he thought safe. He wondered if the shooting was possibly related to the illegal drug trade. Great quantities of drugs were transported on a regular basis from Mexico to the northwest part of the United States. There were so few places to conveniently cross the Colorado River in the vast remoteness that stretched from western Colorado across southeast Utah and down to the Grand Canyon in Arizona. The bridge across the river at Moab was a natural funnel for commercial truck traffic for the same reason the Old Spanish Trail had gone through here. It was one of the few feasible places to cross the river's canyon. The same would be true for drug trafficking. So he postulated the victim's death was likely drug related. Why else would anyone kill a man out in the middle of God's country? Robbery would be unlikely. Maybe a personal matter or a hunting accident. But very possibly a drug deal gone bad.

Soon, the sandstone Fisher Towers came into view. He turned right on the dirt road that followed Onion Creek up to Fisher Valley. The creek was swollen with runoff from the previous day's heavy rains, forcing him to slow to a crawl at each creek crossing. Water-filled potholes in the roadway added to the challenge, the driver never knowing the depth of any given hole. After a half-hour of tedious driving on the Onion Creek Road, he ascended from the floor of the canyon, crested the top of the hill, and arrived at Fisher Valley, now carpeted yellow with snakeweed in bloom. He crossed the valley and drove to the place where Cottonwood Canyon began its long, tortuous descent toward the Dolores River. There, the Kokopelli Trail intersected the head of the canyon.

In the distance he could see two vehicles. The pickup truck with the BLM insignia on the door belonged to Adam Dunne, the Investigative Agent whose jurisdiction covered all BLM land in the southeast Utah quadrant—fifty thousand square miles of wilderness. This generally meant that county sheriffs' departments conducted criminal investigations with the BLM in an assisting role. Rivera had worked with Dunne on several previous cases. He'd found him to be competent, cooperative, and likeable. Dunne, tall and slender with dark hair, lived in Castle Valley with his wife and four children.

The second vehicle was an old Ford pickup that he knew belonged to Doctor Pudge Devlin, part-time Medical Examiner for Grand County and semi-retired general practitioner. Rivera knew him well and enjoyed his company. Devlin had given up a very successful practice in Denver early in life and moved to the Moab area twenty-two years ago. Opting for a slower pace, he'd bought a small farm in Castle Valley where he planted a two-acre vineyard, made his own wine, and now consumed the resulting Merlot on a daily basis. His florid face and the ample belly overhanging his belt were testament to the quality of the product. Since Castle Valley was closer to the crime scene than Moab, both Devlin and Dunne had arrived before Rivera.

Rivera parked his vehicle and approached his colleagues. Three young, brightly-clad bikers sat beside their mountain bikes on a nearby knoll and watched. Devlin was the first to speak.

"Manny, we've got a corpse here, male, Hispanic, mid-twenties. Been dead for twelve to twenty-four hours. Looks like a single bullet wound to the top of the head. I'll have a better estimate of the time of death after I get him back to town and do an autopsy. I've called the funeral home and asked them to send out a vehicle to pick up the corpse."

"Thanks Doc," said Rivera as he approached the body. He observed the black dried blood in the victim's matted hair. The body was lying face down near the side of the trail, one arm folded under the chest, the other extended outward. Aside from the head wound, he could see no other signs of injury. A cowboy hat was stuck on the spiny branches of a nearby blackbrush.

Dunne pointed to the hat. "There's a bullet hole in the top of the hat and some powder burns. Must've been shot at close range."

Rivera studied the hat and nodded in agreement. He returned to his vehicle and retrieved a Nikon digital camera and some yellow crime-scene tape. He cordoned off the area around the body with the tape and then began photographing. There were several sets of footprints—one made by boots and three made by biker's shoes. There were also several bicycle-tire impressions. Dunne said the boot prints likely belonged to Devlin, and, after a quick check by Rivera, this proved to be the case. Dunne himself had been careful not to disturb the area with his own prints. The other prints matched the shoes worn by the young men, and the tire tracks were a match for their bike tires.

Rivera and Dunne interviewed the bikers. They said they were biking the Kokopelli Trail end-to-end, from Moab to Grand Junction, a distance of one-hundred and forty-six miles across some very rugged terrain. They'd camped out last night about two miles to the west. No gun shots had been heard. They'd broken camp at first light and resumed their journey, shortly thereafter finding the corpse by the side of the trail. Checking the man and discovering he was dead, they'd used a cell phone to call the authorities.

The bikers wore dour expressions. They said encountering the corpse during their journey had been a real downer. They were unhappy at the delay, as they had set certain elapsed-time goals for their trip. Rivera recorded their names, addresses, and other particulars in his notepad. He photographed them, their bicycles, and in particular the tread patterns of the tires. He thanked them for their cooperation and told them they were free to go. They hopped on their bikes and resumed their journey. Rivera briefly watched them as they pedaled up the incline, thinking that he too should take up mountain biking. But that would have to wait for another day.

The three men returned to the body and turned it over. It had begun to stiffen with rigor mortis and the skin of the face and hands had become a mottled purple color. They noted the clothing on the victim's back was damp but the front was relatively dry. The ground on which the corpse had rested was also dry.

"It looks like he was shot before the thunderstorms yesterday evening," he said.

Dunne nodded and added, "Yeah, and the rain was real heavy out here. Not much chance of finding the shooter's tracks."

Rivera knelt by the body and began extracting the contents of the victim's pockets. The pockets of the denim jacket produced a pack of Marlboro cigarettes and a plastic sandwich bag containing two marijuana joints. Loose items in the front pockets of the jeans included three keys on a ring, a book of matches from the My-Oh-My Club in Cortez, and forty-seven cents. There were also twenty-six Mexican pesos, all in coins. The back pockets yielded a red and white handkerchief and an old leather wallet containing sixty-six dollars in twenties and singles, a faded photograph of an attractive, older Hispanic woman, and a receipt from the McClane Feed Store in Grand Junction for fifty bags of cattle nutrient pellets. The receipt was made out to the Rutherford Ranch and dated three days earlier. The wallet also contained several discount coupons for various fast-food restaurants and a Texas driver's license. The photograph on the driver's license matched the victim and showed him to be Jesse B. Montoya, 25 years of age, from Harlingen, Texas. Rivera bagged and tagged each item.

Four hours later, after the mortician had picked up the body, both Devlin and Dunne had departed. Rivera now stood alone at the crime scene. The air was still and the high desert quiet. A raven flew overhead on its way down Cottonwood Canyon toward the Dolores River. Rivera could hear the swooshing of its wings even though it was more than two hundred feet above him. As he inspected the area around the crime scene, he wondered how in the world a man gets shot in the top of the head at close range out here in the middle of nowhere. There was nothing in the area except rabbit brush, sage, blackbrush and a dead juniper bleached white by the sun.

He walked over to a shallow sandstone outcropping and sat down. The woman in the photograph came into his thoughts. The dead man's mother? Possibly. If so, she would soon be receiving some terrible news. And why the Mexican pesos in the victim's pocket? Maybe he was a Mexican national, or perhaps a frequent traveler to Mexico. Harlingen wasn't very far from the border. And the joints? Not uncommon, but they certainly suggested some kind of a drug connection. He wondered about the young man. Only 25 years old. Too young to have experienced much of life. What a waste.

As Rivera sat there thinking about the situation, his own limited experience in solving crimes moved to the forefront of his mind. He'd never before been assigned as lead investigator in a murder case. A part of him hoped the sheriff would assign the case to someone else. But if it *were* assigned to him, he knew it would be an opportunity to put into practice some of the things he'd learned pursuing a degree in criminal justice. He wasn't really sure which outcome he preferred. There were no clues at the crime scene except a corpse with a bullet in its head. The area had been scoured by a heavy rainfall, erasing all tracks from the day before. And there was no obvious motive. Certainly robbery could be ruled out as there was cash in the man's pocket. Rivera stood up. He had no idea where to begin the investigation.

He returned to his vehicle and started the long drive back to Moab, deciding not to worry about things too much at this point. He would just wait and see what the sheriff had to say. He picked up the radio handset, raised Millie, and told her he was leaving the area and returning to the office.

"Manny, the sheriff wants to see you as soon as you arrive."

"OK, Millie," he said and signed off. The sheriff would have lots of questions, questions for which Rivera had few answers.

4

RIVERA ARRIVED BACK in Moab by mid-afternoon and parked his vehicle in the lot behind the Grand County Municipal Office Building on Center Street. He entered the two-story, sand-colored brick structure and proceeded directly to the sheriff's office. He knocked on the office door and stepped inside. With his left hand, Sheriff Leroy Bradshaw was pressing his phone against his ear. His right hand was holding a pencil which he impatiently bounced on the yellow pad resting on his desk. He wore an expression of concern. He was a large man, 52-years old, with thinning blond hair combed straight back. He'd been the County Sheriff for twelve years, and had served as a deputy for the previous sixteen. Rivera knew him to be smart, fair, and experienced, a man who'd seen most everything during his career. The sheriff motioned for him to come in and have a seat.

"Yes. Okay. Yes. We're on it. I'll let you know," said Bradshaw and hung up the phone. The sheriff sat there without a word, staring past Rivera at the far wall. Rivera waited for him to speak.

"That was one of the county councilmen," said Bradshaw as he reached for the empty coffee mug on his desk. He stood up and walked over to his coffee maker for a refill.

"Want some, Manny?"

"Yes Sir, thanks," said Rivera, still craving his first cup of the day. Bradshaw brought back two steaming mugs, gave one to his deputy, and lowered himself into the large leather chair behind his walnut desk. Both men sipped their coffee.

"OK, Manny, fill me in," said the sheriff. Rivera spent the next ten minutes summarizing the facts, starting with the 9-1-1 call from the mountain bikers, detailing the crime scene investigation, and ending with the removal of the body.

"Odd location for a homicide," said Bradshaw.

"Another thing that's odd is the entry wound. The victim was shot in the top of the head at close range. He couldn't have been standing when it happened because there's no high vantage point for a shooter in the immediate area."

The sheriff sat there quietly for a moment, his lips pursed, looking down at his desk. Rivera waited, shifting slightly in his chair. Finally, the sheriff spoke. "OK, Manny, this is your case. Drop everything else you're working on. Get whatever help you need from BLM and the state police. Talk to them directly. If you think you need to talk to the FBI, come through me."

Bradshaw took a sip of coffee and continued. "Everyone knows outdoor tourism is the financial life-blood of this county. Draws in tens of thousands of people every year for hiking, rafting, off-road driving, and so forth. I've already gotten calls from three Grand County councilmen, two Moab city councilmen, several local business people, and the motel association representative. This kind of news travels fast. They've all heard about the killing and they're worried about the negative impact it'll have on tourism. Who would want to hike the LaSal Mountains knowing there's a killer on the loose out there? We've got to solve this ASAP. So get right on it, and let me know what help you need. And keep me posted. Questions?"

There being none, Rivera left the sheriff, walked to his small office down the hall, and sat down at his desk. He reflected on his new assignment and the things that needed to be done. Then he got to work. First, he typed a report which outlined what had happened thus far in the case while the events of the day were still fresh in his mind. That finished, he ran the identities of the three bikers through the National Law Enforcement Database searching for wants and warrants, and any history of criminal activity. He expected none and got none. They had seemed like solid citizens but everything had to be checked. Then he turned his attention to the victim. The contents of Jesse Montoya's wallet had included his driver's license with an address in Texas. He contacted the Texas Department of Public Safety and the Cameron County Sheriff's Department. Neither could find any record of Montoya. The driver's license was obviously bogus. Maybe the victim's name was an alias. Rivera decided to run Montoya's fingerprints and identity through the FBI's database to see if they produced any hits. That would take some time.

Next, he spread the contents of Montoya's pockets out on his desk. There wasn't much to go on. Even the fast-food discount coupons had expired. The only thing that looked useful was the receipt from the McClane Feed Store made out to the Rutherford Ranch. Rivera was vaguely familiar with the ranch, having once met the foreman Paul Williamson and his wife Sarah at a fund raiser for the benefit of the Moab Home for Needy Children. Rivera was acquainted with the Williamsons mostly by reputation. They were highly regarded by the Moab locals for their hard work and financial support of the children's home. After that first meeting, Rivera had seen them around Moab on occasion and exchanged greetings, but he didn't know them well.

He looked up the phone number for the ranch and dialed it. Sarah Williamson answered. After some polite preliminaries, Rivera asked to speak to Mr. Williamson.

"Oh, I'm sorry, Deputy Rivera. Paul is in Cortez attending a cattle auction and isn't due back until the day after tomorrow."

"I see. Perhaps you could help me, Mrs. Williamson. Is there a man named Jesse Montoya employed at the ranch?"

"Yes, there is. He's been working here for a few months. I'm afraid I don't know him very well. Is there a problem?"

"Mrs. Williamson, I have some very bad news. Jesse is dead. His body was found up near Fisher Valley this morning. He was shot in the head."

"Oh, my word! What happened?" She sounded distraught and shocked.

"We don't know yet. The investigation is just getting under way. We have very little information at this time." Rivera paused. "I'm sorry for your loss." Another pause. "Could you put Mr. Rutherford on the phone?"

"Mr. Rutherford won't be able to come to the phone." She lowered her voice to a whisper. "He's quite old and speaks very little. I'm afraid he's showing signs of dementia."

Rivera made an appointment to come to the ranch in the morning to interview the other ranch hands. He also wanted to look at Montoya's personal effects. He hung up the phone, hoping tomorrow he would produce information that would shed some light on

Montoya's life. Maybe he could back-track the man's history and find a possible motive for the killing.

He stared at the two marijuana joints on his desk. When he was a rookie cop in his home town of Las Cruces, New Mexico, the majority of the arrests he made had been related in some way to illegal drugs. Or alcohol. The same was true here in Grand County. Why do people find it necessary to use these substances when the beauty of the high desert and endless skies are more than enough to elevate one's spirits? That thought always puzzled him.

Dr. Devlin and Adam Dunne converged on the Sheriff's Department at the same time. They entered Rivera's office and sat down in the grey visitor's chairs. Dunne spoke first. "We've issued an advisory to all local BLM, Forest Service, and National Park Service personnel describing the shooting and requesting they be on the lookout for anything suspicious in the backcountry.

Rivera knew it was unlikely the advisory would produce a viable lead, but all bases had to be covered.

"Sorry, Manny," Dunne went on, "but I've got to bug out on you. There's a planned demonstration by an environmental group protesting the reopening of a copper mine down in Lisbon Valley. An informant tipped us that a few radical members of the group are planning to sabotage the mining equipment in the morning. I want to get in place tonight and be ready to stop it before it starts. You know how those things can get out of hand."

Rivera updated him on what he had learned about Montoya thus far, after which Dunne departed.

Then it was Devlin's turn. "Time of death was about 2:00 P.M. yesterday, give or take an hour," he said as he handed a clear plastic evidence bag to Rivera. The bag contained a single nine-millimeter slug. "This was definitely the cause of death. Found it imbedded in the brain stem, just above the atlas vertebra. A single shot to the top of the head, as though the shooter were standing directly above the victim. Very unusual angle. Straight down. The body had no bruises and showed no signs of a struggle."

Rivera took the bag and inspected the slug.

"There's more, Manny," continued Devlin. "You know what a potsherd is, don't you?"

"Sure. It's a fragment from a broken pot. Usually refers to a piece from an Ancient Indian pot."

"Right. Well, I found a small potsherd stuck into the victim's chest. A shallow penetration, through the shirt, and just barely into the skin." He handed a second evidence bag to Rivera. It contained a white sherd with two black linear markings. The fragment was wedge shaped, about an inch long and a quarter-inch wide at the base. Rivera held the bag up and studied the sherd. Puzzled, he looked back at Devlin.

"The second thing I found was small traces of high quality cocaine in the victim's nostrils."

"So the guy was certainly a serious doper," said Rivera. "This sure looks like a drug case. But I'm having a hard time getting a picture of just how the killing took place. For example, there's no place at the crime scene for a shooter to hide and fire directly down at his target." He considered that for a moment. "I guess it's possible the shooter wasn't hiding at all. Maybe the victim and shooter knew each other. In that case, the victim might have been on his knees. Maybe he got shot execution style." He thought some more. "Or maybe the shooting took place somewhere else and afterwards the body was moved."

Rivera massaged his chin. "The potsherd is strange. Pot fragments are fairly common in this part of the country, but I didn't see any others at the crime scene. If this one had just been lying out there by the side of the trail, it would probably have been found and removed long ago by a hiker or biker. That's illegal, of course, but it happens. I'll go back out to the site tomorrow and take another look around."

"OK, Manny, I'll get a copy of my written report over here tomorrow, but I wanted you to know right away what I'd found so far. I'll arrange to have the body shipped to the State Medical Examiner up in Salt Lake City in the morning. They'll do a final autopsy but I doubt they'll find anything else. Let me know if there's anything more I can do."

"Many thanks, Doc."

Alone again, Rivera considered what he had. Which wasn't much. He'd probably gotten all the evidence he was going to get from the body. Tomorrow morning at the ranch he would learn more about Jesse Montoya. Then he would revisit the crime scene looking for pot-sherds or anything he might have missed during his sweep of the area this morning. He decided he would hike the Kokopelli Trail for a half-mile in each direction from the place where Montoya's body had been found to see if he could find anything unusual.

Rivera spent the remainder of the day supplementing his report with his analysis of the contents of Montoya's pockets, the results of the driver's license check, his conversation with Sarah Williamson, and the findings of the Medical Examiner. He transmitted Montoya's fingerprints and other pertinent facts to the FBI requesting any information they had on the victim. It was now late evening.

On his way home, Rivera ran his vehicle through the carwash. Then he stopped at City Market, the local grocery store, to buy some dinner at the deli counter. He was famished and in need of a hot meal, having eaten only granola bars all day. A couple of burritos would do the trick. As they were being wrapped, he glanced over at the salad bar where a smiling young couple was assembling take-out salads for dinner. They looked slim and healthy and reminded him he needed to improve his diet. But for right now the thought of burritos made him salivate. Eating right would have to wait for another day.

Back home, after he fed the guppies, he sat at the kitchen table eating the burritos and washing them down with a cold bottle of Budweiser. He reflected on what he knew about the murder, and particularly all the things he didn't know. A mild sense of despair began gnawing at his self-confidence. What if he couldn't solve the case? Bradshaw would certainly be disappointed. He was a fair man, so Rivera didn't think failure would cost him his job—but it was possible. He loved his work and he loved living in the Moab area. He had to do much better with this assignment than the last one the sheriff had entrusted to him. He was embarrassed as he remembered it.

One month ago, Bradshaw had assigned him to an important stakeout. A small marijuana garden had been discovered by a lone hiker near Yellow Cat Wash on BLM land just north of Arches National Park. The hiker, an older man, had stopped to rest near the wash when he heard some rustling of the brush in a side arroyo. He went to investigate. When he pushed through the brush, he spotted two ground squirrels scampering away and three rows of meticulously cultivated marijuana plants. Having been a user in his youth during the sixties, he recognized the plants immediately and reported the find to the authorities. Rivera was assigned to stake out the plot and apprehend the rogue cultivators when they returned to harvest the plants. One afternoon, while he was observing the illicit crop from his hiding place in the high ground of an area called Eagle Park, he heard two gunshots from within Arches National Park. He immediately left his post to investigate. When he returned an hour later after seeing no one, the entire crop had been harvested. He realized then he'd been spotted staking out the marijuana plot and the gunshots were simply a diversion created by the harvesters to induce him to leave the area. Explaining all this to the sheriff had not been one of his favorite law enforcement moments.

During his meeting with Bradshaw earlier in the day, the sheriff seemed to have thought long and hard before assigning such an important case to a relatively junior man. All of the more experienced deputies had been tied up on other pressing matters. Probably Bradshaw had chosen him with a certain amount of discomfort and doubt. And who could blame him? It was clear to Rivera he had to be successful this time.

5

SORENSON SAT HIDDEN among the boulders and watched from his now-familiar perch atop a remote bluff in the Dark Canyon Wilderness Area. He looked south across Cedar Mesa, a vast landscape southwest of Blanding consisting of several hundred square miles of rolling table-top land. The mesa was dark green with its cover of pinyon pines and junipers, except in those places where it was sliced by a labyrinth of rugged canyons. The air was cool and crystal clear.

He watched three buzzards circling in the distance, rising effortlessly on a thermal updraft. A narrow dirt road came toward him from the horizon, patiently winding its way across the mesa top, circuitously skirting the deep canyons. The road passed two hundred feet directly below him on its way to a remote part of the Dark Canyon Plateau, where its quality diminished, eventually becoming two tracks through the sagebrush and finally fading into non-existence. This was the road that would be used by the Indian artifact dealer from Farmington to arrive at their agreed-upon rendezvous point. Here, Indian pots and figurines would be exchanged for cash.

It was a secluded location with little if any traffic, and from where he was situated, Sorenson could see if the dealer was alone in his SUV and whether he was being followed. Vehicles on dry dirt roads created dust plumes which could be seen for miles—driving undetected was virtually impossible.

He'd parked his pickup atop the bluff behind a cluster of pinyon pines just off a dirt road that had no connection with the road below. The two men had performed this ritual several times before and it had always come off as planned. As a precaution, and unbeknownst to the dealer, Sorenson had made a practice of arriving an hour early to wait and watch. This time was no exception.

Earlier in the morning, he'd arisen from a night of fitful sleep, left the motel in Blanding, and gone to his storage unit a few blocks away. He retrieved the pots in their bubble-wrap protection and placed them in a cardboard box, using wadded-up newspaper as padding and securing the lid with a single piece of masking tape. He placed the box on a foam pad on the passenger-side floor of his truck and concealed it with a blanket. He placed the Glock, its magazine, and bullets in the glove compartment. He tossed a plastic laundry bag containing his clothing and boots from the previous day on the seat. Then, he transferred his

Barrett sniper rifle and its scope into the vehicle, each in its own wooden case. Lastly, he retrieved an unregistered Smith and Wesson 360 PD revolver that he kept in his storage unit. This would replace the Glock he was about to dispose of.

After leaving the storage unit, he'd driven first to the Blanding public dump. It was deserted. He'd hidden the shirt, pants, socks, and boots in separate places under vast piles of black plastic bags filled with kitchen garbage, lawn clippings and other forms of modern detritus. Afterwards he'd taken Highway 95 to its intersection with Highway 276 and continued on to the ferry landing at Hall's Crossing. He'd waited there for a half-hour until loading began for the voyage across Lake Powell. The small vessel was capable of carrying a dozen vehicles, but this morning there were only two: his pickup truck and a late-model white Buick driven by an older couple. After the ferry pulled away from shore and began its journey to Bullfrog Landing on the opposite side of the lake, he removed the Glock, magazine, and bullets from his glove compartment and stuffed them in his pockets. He exited the truck and walked along the side railing until he reached a place where the ship's superstructure blocked the crew's view of him. The older couple remained in their car. He dumped the incriminating evidence into the lake, hoping everything would sink into the sandy bottom and be gone forever.

Later, he took the return trip on the ferry, proceeded back to Highway 95, and drove east. He turned left on the road into Natural Bridges National Monument. After a short distance, he turned right and continued for several miles on a winding dirt road. As he neared his destination, he slowed to a crawl as the road became rocky and precarious. A sheer drop-off on his left and a rising bluff on his right caused him to tighten his grip on the steering wheel. He carefully circumvented the arroyos which had been cut by torrents of water which cascaded over the cliff during rainstorms. Finally reaching the rendezvous point, he switched off the engine, exited the truck, and stood there, watching and listening. Minutes passed. Only after satisfying himself he was alone did he remove the box from the truck.

He walked through the sagebrush toward the bluff and arrived at a large rock about fifteen feet from the road. He placed the box behind the rock. Then he glanced upward at the pile of boulders which ascended to the top of the bluff. Shading his eyes with his hand, he located the place where he would later be hiding and watching. He returned to his truck, started the engine, and drove until he reached a place where the road was wide enough to turn the vehicle around. He retraced his route back to the pavement, drove south a short distance, and turned left onto a dirt road. An hour of driving on backcountry dirt roads brought him to the top of the bluff, the place where he now waited and kept watch over the box.

He sat there, cradling his rifle. Though it had been many years since his Army days, it was a familiar and comfortable feeling. He opened the fore and aft covers protecting the scope's optics and scanned the mesa. Then he aimed downward and inspected the area below him. The view of the box was unobstructed. It was a perfect place for an exchange and it had worked well each time before. He raised the scope and followed the road as far as he could toward the horizon. He saw no activity. Good. In another hour, a green Jeep Rubicon would come into view. The dealer had always been prompt and followed his instructions with a precision that Sorenson liked.

As he waited, he began reflecting on the deal he'd made with Donald Twitchell, owner and proprietor of Twitchell's Indian Artifacts on West Broadway Street in Farmington, New Mexico. He'd learned of the man from a newspaper article he read two months ago in the Arts section of the Sunday *Salt Lake Tribune*. The feature article described Twitchell as a smart and prosperous artifact dealer, well known to collectors and museums from coast to coast. The accompanying color picture showed an older man, florid-faced, bald and overweight. But there was something about the man's blue eyes that caught Sorenson's attention. They had a look which suggested intelligence, intensity, and cunning. The article had been flattering of Twitchell, with words of praise from several prominent collectors and a museum curator on the East Coast. He was known as an expert appraiser, trader, and retailer of Indian artifacts.

The last part of the lengthy article indicated that Twitchell had been questioned several times by the FBI regarding possible violations of the American Antiquities Act of 1906. The act forbade removal of Indian artifacts from federal lands and Indian reservations unless specific written permission had been obtained from the government. But the regulations didn't apply to artifacts recovered from private lands, so a cottage industry producing false provenance documents had sprung up. Items illicitly recovered were often accompanied by documents certifying they were discovered on private lands. Twitchell was reputed to be an expert at falsifying such documents, according to an unidentified "reliable" source, but nothing had ever been proven.

As Sorenson waited and watched, he remembered how he had made contact with Twitchell and set up their business arrangement without Twitchell ever laying eyes on him or knowing anything about him. The day after he'd read the *Tribune* article and several weeks after he'd found the cave and its treasure, he called Twitchell from a pay phone in Salt Lake City. He told him he'd recently discovered a large collection of old pots and figurines in excellent condition and wanted to sell them a few at a time on a cash basis. There were no papers to accompany the artifacts. Twitchell, sounding cautious, laughed and said that sounded quite illegal. How could he possibly know where the pots had come from? Sorenson told Twitchell they came from private land and that there were several dozen of them.

"Several dozen?" inquired Twitchell.

Sorenson said yes and to prove he was serious, he would place one of the pots in a box along with photographs of the rest and a price list, and leave the box at a predetermined secret location. The pot in the box would be Twitchell's to keep, a sign of good faith. He told Twitchell he would call back in a couple of days to see if the trader had any interest. Then he hung up. Sorenson had waited longer than a couple of days, just to let Twitchell stew for a while. Enough time for caution to be brushed aside by greed.

Five days later, he called Twitchell from the same pay phone.

"Any interest in the box we talked about?"

"Yes," said Twitchell without hesitation.

Sorenson gave the dealer directions for locating the box and instructed him to arrive there in three days at exactly 2:00 P.M. It was the same place he was now observing from above, the rendezvous point they'd used ever since.

On that first appointed day and time, the dealer had driven to the agreed-upon spot and retrieved the box. He'd opened it, stared into the box for a moment, then closed it quickly. He carried the box back to his Jeep and drove off. Sorenson had observed everything from his hiding place on top of the bluff. The next day he'd called the dealer.

"You picked up the box. Were the contents satisfactory?"

"Yes indeed," Twitchell said without hesitation. "How do we proceed?"

"You have photographs of the artifacts and a corresponding list of prices. I can sell you three pieces at a time and can make a delivery as often as every three days."

"That's a lot of merchandise to move and represents a large cash outlay. I wouldn't be able to finance the whole deal with my own cash. To manage the cash flow, I'll have to find buyers as I go along."

After some further discussion, they agreed the artifact dealer would secure customers on the basis of the photographs, and the next time Sorenson called, Twitchell would identify by number the three items he wanted delivered.

"Any problem with the price list?" Sorenson asked. He had researched the values of the individual pots and figurines using library resources and the internet. The prices were set at a level he knew would be attractive to

Twitchell, leaving the dealer with more than enough room to make a good profit on each piece.

"No problem at all," Twitchell replied.

Three days after that conversation, Sorenson had called Twitchell to see if any sales had been made. The dealer had buyers for three of the items. The item numbers were provided and the date for the exchange was set. Sorenson assumed Twitchell would forge the provenance papers but didn't ask—that was none of his business. Before he hung up, Sorenson added he would be high in the rocks above the exchange point watching through a scope attached to a high-powered rifle. "You are to come alone, pick up the box containing the three items, leave the money in a paper bag, and depart. And there'd better not be a second vehicle following you in. And after you leave, I'll descend the rocks and check the money. If it's missing or short, there's plenty of time for me to climb back up to the top of the bluff and put a bullet through your windshield. There'll be an opportunity at each switchback."

Twitchell said he understood, the deal was good for him, and there would be no problems. Once again, greed had trumped fear.

The first exchange had gone without a hitch, Sorenson later depositing the cash in a large Salt Lake City bank. Four subsequent sales had also taken place without any problems, the resulting proceeds being spread over accounts in three banks. Each exchange had taken place with a satisfying precision.

As Sorenson reflected on what he'd achieved, he felt the same sense of satisfaction he'd experienced during his Army days in Southeast Asia. The feeling of returning from a successful covert mission, all objectives accomplished. The pots-for-cash operation was complex, challenging, and risky, but he'd been able to pull it off and was now becoming rich.

Then his thoughts turned to the ranch hand he'd killed yesterday. His pride slowly melted into regret. The sight of the rifle in his hands amplified the regret and transformed it into shame. A new thought occurred to him. He realized that Twitchell, while probably dishonest as an artifact dealer, had been true to their agreement and would likely continue to be reliable. The more he thought about it, the more it became clear there was really no need for the rifle anymore. He got up, walked back to his truck, put the rifle and scope back in their cases and left them there. He returned with a pair of binoculars to his lookout point, feeling better about things. And if, one day, the dealer took the box of pots and left no cash, he would simply stop dealing with him and seek another outlet. Severing the relationship would be clean and risk free. After all, Twitchell had no idea who he was. And losing three pots would be quite tolerable compared to the grief of another killing.

It was a warm day. He took a drink of water from a plastic bottle and peered through the binoculars. In the distance, a plume of dust rose from the road. A green Jeep Rubicon slowly came into view. Twitchell, right on time.

The swap took place with the usual precision, the money was correct, and Sorenson returned to Salt Lake City a wealthier man. The next day, he deposited the cash into one of his bank accounts. The total of the three accounts had now risen to $221,300. He decided to lay low and rest for a day. Tomorrow he would call Twitchell and find out when he'd be ready for another delivery.

6

RIVERA GRIPPED THE steering wheel of his Ford F-150 with both hands as he negotiated the switchbacks of the gravel road that descended John Brown Canyon. He'd departed Moab early in the morning and driven east across the Castleton-Gateway Road, traversing the north side of the LaSal Mountains. His destination was the Rutherford Ranch.

As he exited the canyon, the road transitioned to pavement and he entered the tiny hamlet of Gateway, Colorado, on the Dolores River. After a few hundred yards, he left the pavement and drove north, bouncing up the dirt road that followed along the west bank of the Dolores River. Crossing the state line once again, he re-entered Utah. At 9:30 A.M. he reached the main gate of the Rutherford Ranch and continued toward the ranch house, surveying the ranch as he drove. The registered Hereford cattle grazing in the pastures appeared well-fed and healthy. The fencing was straight and the barbed wire taut. Weeds growing along the fence lines had recently been shredded. A large peach orchard along the river was equipped with irrigation pipes and the trees had recently been pruned. The ranch road on which he drove was smooth and graded. It had the look of a well-run outfit. A tribute to the foreman Paul Williamson, he concluded.

Rivera brought his vehicle to a stop in front of the ranch house. He got out, closed the door, and looked up at the old man in the rocking chair on the porch. Rivera had heard about Mr. Rutherford but had never before laid eyes on him. The old man was wearing faded jeans, house slippers, a brown cardigan sweater, and an old cowboy hat.

"Good Morning, Mr. Rutherford." There was no reply, no acknowledgement of the deputy's presence. The man slowly rocked back and forth, his watery blue eyes staring straight ahead, as if locked onto something in the distance. Just then, Sarah Williamson opened the front door and stepped out onto the porch. Rivera was still looking at the old man, waiting for a response.

Mrs. Williamson smiled. "Good morning, Deputy." Then she paused, and seeing Rivera's perplexed expression, she added, "He doesn't say much anymore." The deputy nodded and touched the brim of his hat. "Good morning, Mrs. Williamson. Thanks for seeing me."

"Please call me Sarah," she said with a friendly smile. "Come on in. There's a fresh pot of coffee inside." Rivera judged Sarah to be in her early forties. She was about five-foot-seven, attractive, slender, and poised.

She had light brown shoulder-length hair and wore jeans and a flowery purple blouse. A small turquoise nugget hung from a silver chain around her neck.

Rivera removed his hat and followed her into the large rustic home. The main part of the dwelling appeared to be at least a century old, with several wings added on in more recent times. The air inside was cool and smelled of breakfast. The furnishings consisted of antique hand-hewn pieces. Ranch memorabilia and old tintype portrait photographs in wooden frames decorated the walls. The environment reminded Rivera of his boyhood home in Las Cruces and produced a brief wave of nostalgia. His thoughts flashed to the small, sparsely furnished house he rented in Moab. For an instant, he felt a twinge of emptiness. He forced his focus back to the job at hand. Sarah invited him to sit down at the kitchen table. She filled two white mugs with hot coffee.

"Have you had breakfast? We've got plenty of food here."

"Thanks very much, but yes, I ate at the diner before driving over."

"How about a sweet roll?"

"I've always got room for a sweet roll. Thanks."

They sat there drinking coffee and talking. The conversation was comfortable and unforced. Sarah had a natural smile. They discussed life on the ranch, his job as a deputy sheriff in Moab, and the beauty of

the LaSal Mountains. Rivera consumed two homemade sweet rolls, one with apple filling and one laced
with cinnamon. This is the life, he thought to himself.
They continued making small talk for a while, Rivera
asking about the Moab Home for Needy Children and
Sarah telling him about their successful fund raiser
to replace the leaky roof on the main building. There
was a contagious enthusiasm in her voice as she spoke
about the kids who lived there and the future projects
which were planned.

"As soon as we can raise sufficient funds, we'll start
construction on a second dormitory."

"The whole community is grateful for the fine work
you're doing. Everyone has noticed the improvements
at the home," said Rivera.

"My husband and I sort of adopted the children's
home many years ago as our contribution to the community. Those kids have had tough lives—abused,
abandoned, neglected. I just want them to feel loved
and protected. Fortunately, we've had lots of help from
volunteers and contributors in the Moab area."

Rivera was impressed with Sarah's commitment and
dedication. He would have been interested in learning
more about the home but it was time to shift topics.
"I'm sorry about the loss of your ranch hand. We found
Montoya's body yesterday near the top of Cottonwood
Canyon at the Kokopelli Trail crossing. From the pre-
liminary autopsy, we estimate he was shot and killed

the day before yesterday sometime in the afternoon. I'd like to find out as much about him as I can."

Sarah's facial expression transformed from cheerful to troubled. She spoke haltingly. "I didn't know Jesse well. He'd only worked here for a few months. He was quiet, sort of standoffish. He was always very polite to me, but never really said much. And there wasn't a lot of eye contact. He didn't mix socially with the ranch hands. As I understand it, he spent his days off somewhere down in New Mexico. The other hands referred to him as a loner. But he was considered a good worker."

She thought for a moment and added "We keep a personnel folder on each employee. I'll get Jesse's for you." She slid her chair back, got up, and walked down the hall to an office. Rivera heard the sound of a file drawer opening and closing. She returned with a manila folder and handed it to him. "It contains an application form, a photocopy of his social security card and driver's license, a history of his paychecks and tax withholding, and a Polaroid photograph of him taken on the day he hired on." Rivera opened it and thumbed through the contents as Sarah refilled the coffee mugs. After a cursory inspection, he concluded that there was little useful information in the file. He already knew the driver's license was bogus and surmised that the same was probably true of the social security card. He considered the former employers Montoya had listed on the application. All were located in Texas except the most recent which was a ranch in Cimarron, New Mexico.

"Did you obtain references from the former employers Montoya listed on the application?"

"No. Normally we do that, but in this case, we needed help right away and both Paul and I sized him up as a good young man. He didn't have a lot of experience, but we were short-handed so we just hired him on the spot."

"How did he arrive at the ranch?"

"He came on his motorcycle. He'd seen our handwritten help-wanted ad at the general store in Gateway. His motorcycle is parked behind the bunkhouse under a tarp."

"Before I leave, I'll need to take a look at the motorcycle and his room in the bunkhouse."

"Of course," said Sarah.

"How many employees do you currently have working here?"

"Eddie Stokes, our top hand, and three others, not counting Jesse. Eddie's been here the longest, about four years, the others less. All of them are great employees. Hard workers. Not a trouble maker in the bunch. My husband can tell you more about them. He'll be back from Cortez tomorrow, but meanwhile you're welcome to look at their personnel files too."

Rivera considered that. "If it's OK with you, I'd like to take all the personnel files back to the office.

I'll make copies and return the originals to you in a couple of days."

Sarah went back to the office, retrieved the files, and gave them to Rivera.

He thanked her. "I'd like to talk to Eddie Stokes now if he's available."

"Certainly. I think he's working out in the equipment barn. I'll go get him."

"No, that's okay — I don't want to take any more of your time than necessary. I'll go find him." He thanked Sarah for her hospitality, picked up the personnel folders, and left the ranch house. He put the folders in his vehicle.

He found Eddie in the equipment barn, lying on his back, tinkering with something on the underside of an old GMC pickup truck. Eddie slid out from under the vehicle and stood up. He wiped his hands with an oily red rag. Rivera took a mental snapshot of the man. Eddie was about forty, medium height, with auburn hair, hazel eyes, and a ruddy complexion. He was wearing faded jeans with holes in the knees, a well-worn green cowboy shirt with grease stains, and an old pair of work boots. Rivera introduced himself and began by asking Eddie what he knew about Montoya.

Rivera took notes as Stokes spoke. He learned that Montoya was a good worker who followed orders, a loner, and a probable dope user. "We could smell marijuana on his clothes when he returned from his days off. The other ranch hands told me about it, but the guy was a good employee, so I didn't question him. He never gave us a reason to complain about anything."

"Did Montoya ever talk about his private life, where he was from, what he did on his days off, that sort of thing?"

"Not really. He was pretty quiet. Didn't mix much. When he did talk, it was about cattle, fence-building, saddles, you know, things related to his job. He asked a lot of questions about ranching and seemed to be trying to learn from the experienced hands. I think he was trying to improve himself." Eddie opened a can of oil and began refilling the truck's crankcase. "Aside from the pot-smoking business, he was a good hand. Inexperienced in many ways, but he carried his weight."

"What can you tell me about what happened here the day before yesterday?"

"I was talking to Paul Williamson in front of the ranch house. It was early afternoon, about one thirty, I think. We saw Jesse's horse come back to the ranch house without Jesse in the saddle. He was supposed to be up in Cottonwood Canyon—that's on the west end of the ranch—looking for strays. At first we thought it was funny, you know, his horse just trotting off and leaving him stranded, but then we realized he might be hurt. So Paul drove up there in his pickup looking for him. He came back empty-handed just before dark. I went up there the next morning and looked some more but there was no sign of Jesse. Then we heard he'd been found shot, a few miles outside the ranch boundary. I have no idea what he was doing way out there."

Rivera found the road across the ranch that led to Cottonwood Canyon and headed in that direction. He'd learned little of any use from the other three ranch hands. And the search of Montoya's quarters was equally fruitless. He'd found nothing but clothing, toiletries, and two well-worn paperback novels printed in Spanish. The saddlebags on his motorcycle were empty except for a couple of water bottles, an oily rag, and some tools. Rivera turned right at a fork in the road and entered the gaping mouth of Cottonwood Canyon.

The road in the canyon was barely a road, but it was the quickest way from the ranch house to the Kokopelli Trail. He shifted his thoughts to the crime scene. His plan was to inspect the area more thoroughly, especially along the trail itself. It was the potsherd that puzzled him. He wanted to know if there were other sherds in the area, particularly the same type that had been found penetrating the victim's skin. Maybe that would tell him something useful, though he wasn't really certain how it would help.

He stopped his vehicle and extracted the *Moab East* map from his vehicle door pocket. It was a detailed mountain biking and recreation map published by Latitude 40 Degrees that showed the back roads and topology of eastern Grand County. That map, along with its companion map *Moab West*, were the two he found most useful in his day-to-day activities.

He unfolded the map and carefully spread it out on the passenger-side seat. That done, he resumed driving slowly up the canyon. Sheer red rock walls loomed silently on each side. Streaks of desert varnish, the result of minerals leached out of the sandstone by seeping water, gave portions of the walls a black sheen. The grey-green sage that populated the edges of the canyon floor was covered with small purple blossoms, spurred by the recent rains. The various grasses which grew there were now beginning to turn golden as the nights became cooler. Chunks of red rock, having fallen off the cliffs long ago, decorated the canyon floor along with a smattering of dark green junipers. He consulted his map and compass periodically in order to monitor his progress up the canyon and understand more about the geography of the area.

After a half hour of bumping and lurching up the road, Rivera passed the mouth of Burro Canyon on his left, a tributary which, during a hard rain, would empty its contents into the main canyon. He continued driving, his hands tight on the steering wheel, and his gaze alternating between the beauty up ahead and the rocks in the road that threatened the undercarriage of his vehicle.

He passed the mouth of another tributary which, according to his map, was called Seven Mile Canyon.

It connected to the main canyon from his right. Soon thereafter, he rattled across the cattle guard which marked the Rutherford Ranch boundary and the beginning of BLM land.

A mile beyond the cattle guard, he passed the mouth of Thompson Canyon on his left. A small herd of mule deer grazing there looked up and stared at him. A frightened fawn skittered a few feet, then huddled close to its mother, peering with large inquisitive eyes at the noisy steel creature laboring up the main canyon. Finally, after an hour of wrestling with the steering wheel, Rivera reached the top of Cottonwood Canyon, the place where it intersected with the Kokopelli Trail and where the body of Jesse Montoya had been found. He stopped the vehicle, got out and stretched, arching his back and bending from side to side. It was late afternoon. Cool air descended from the mountains and the sky was clear. He took a drink of water, locked his vehicle and began his trek.

His plan was to hike along the Kokopelli Trail a half-mile in each direction from where the body had been found. He would search for anything unusual, particularly the presence of potsherds. He started out in a northeasterly direction, his eyes focused on the ground. His gaze scanned from side to side taking in a swath that included not only the trail itself but also a few feet on each side. After proceeding a quarter-mile up the trail and finding nothing out of the ordinary, he stopped for a moment to rest his eyes. A yellow-breasted western meadowlark was perched on the branch of a dead juniper tree up ahead. It warbled its flute-like song and flew off. The high desert was quiet again except for the rustling of tall grass tufts moving in the light breeze. He took another drink of water from the plastic bottle he carried and resumed his search. He approached a tumbleweed which had been pinned by the wind against a prickly-pear cactus. A greenish-grey collared lizard with a bright yellow head emerged from beneath it and darted across his path. It stopped abruptly, looked up, and stared at the interloper in the tan uniform. Rivera froze and watched. The lizard considered him for a moment, then turned away and sprinted off, its hind legs throwing tiny puffs of sand into the air as it headed for the safety of its burrow. The deputy smiled and resumed his hike.

After searching the trail for a half-mile, he'd found nothing. He returned to his starting point and examined the trail for a half-mile in the other direction. Again, nothing. He wasn't really surprised. If there had been some potsherds along the way, hikers would likely have collected them by now. And that, he realized as he returned to his starting point, was what made the sherd found stuck into Montoya's chest so peculiar.

He sat down on a lichen-covered rock on a grassy knoll near his vehicle and pondered. What would Bradshaw do? When he was a deputy, the sheriff had developed a reputation for being a top-notch detective. He had solved half a dozen crimes the department had all but abandoned as unsolvable. Bradshaw's reputation had spread, and soon he was lecturing at law academies on fact verification, logic, and inference. Rivera hoped someday he'd be as good a cop as his boss. He reflected on what he'd found so far. There was no suspect and no clear motive. All he had was a corpse, a slug, and a potsherd. The dead man had been a ranch hand, a drug user, and maybe a drug dealer. His driver's license had been falsified, something not typically done by a solid citizen. Somehow Rivera needed to determine Montoya's real identity. He decided that when he returned to the office, he would not only check the references listed on Montoya's employment application, but would also run background checks on all the other ranch employees. He'd check on Paul and Sarah Williamson as well. Even old Mr. Rutherford. And he'd run Montoya's photograph through the FBI's database.

Rivera watched a red-tailed hawk flying low in the distance, scanning the ground for anything that moved. He wondered how he would report his progress to the sheriff at the end of the day. He was a little intimidated by Bradshaw, like any employee is of any boss, but he also admired the man. And he wanted to please him. Actually, Rivera admitted to himself, he wanted to *impress* Bradshaw. He knew the sheriff was under a lot of pressure from the community to solve this crime, and that produced in Rivera an even greater sense of urgency.

Time passed. The longer he sat there in the vast stillness, the less he thought about potsherds. It was as if his mind had subconsciously decided to take a break from its struggles. He began to focus on the natural wonders that surrounded him. Here were ancient sedimentary deposits and volcanic intrusions that had been sculpted and eroded by wind and water and time into a landscape of almost frightening beauty, a huge sky that overwhelmed his sense of self, and clear fresh air that made breathing deeply an enjoyable sensory experience. But most of all, the high desert country had an exquisite silence that Rivera loved. It relaxed him, both physically and mentally. He allowed himself a few minutes to let the tranquility soak in.

He recalled the first time he'd visited the Moab area as a boy. He was a sophomore in high school and the whole class had been taken to Canyonlands National Park on a school bus. He remembered stepping off the bus and becoming instantly and forever hooked on the enormous red rock wilderness. As an adult, he'd visited Moab once or twice every year, each trip producing a kind of spiritual renewal within him. He developed a yearning to live full time in the area. After four years on the city police force in Las Cruces, he applied for a deputy's position in Grand County and got the job.

That was two years ago. It had been difficult moving away from family and friends, but he'd finally fulfilled his dream. His thoughts were interrupted by the sound of voices in the distance.

He stood up and looked around. Hiking toward him from the south rim of Cottonwood Canyon were four young adults, two men and two women. They seemed to be a happy group, talking and laughing the way young people do. As they approached the man in uniform, they became subdued. Then one of the girls said something Rivera couldn't hear, and they all started laughing again.

The young man wearing jeans and a long sleeve T-shirt that said *Get High on Life* spoke first.

"Hi, Officer."

"Hi. Great day for a hike," Rivera said. They all smiled and nodded in agreement.

"We're letterboxing," said the pretty blonde wearing khaki shorts and a white University of Colorado sweat shirt. Her pony tail was threaded through the adjustment strap on the back of her pink cap. She smiled, as if waiting for the officer to show some sign that he was impressed.

"What's letterboxing?" asked Rivera, hoping he didn't sound hopelessly uninformed.

The other girl chimed in. "I can't believe you haven't heard of it," she said, her smile revealing braces. She was a redhead with freckles and wore olive drab shorts and a long sleeve faded yellow shirt. "We're searching for small boxes hidden up here in the mountains. The clues to finding the boxes are located on internet websites devoted to people interested in letterboxing. In each box is a notepad where you add your name, the date, and your hometown to a list of previous visitors. There's also a rubber stamp in each box with an icon that's unique to that site. You stamp the icon into your letterboxing journal to prove you actually found the site, then enter the date, who you were with, and any other information you want to add." She handed Rivera her own journal. He paged through it, was genuinely impressed, and said so.

The second young man, a studious-looking fellow with shoulder-length brown hair and wire-rim glasses, spoke. "Letterboxing originated in England. It combines the fun of hiking with the challenge of a treasure hunt. Lots of people do it. And there are lots of letterboxes hidden right here in the Moab area."

"Sounds like fun. I'd like to try it sometime," said Rivera. And he meant it.

The first young man spoke again. "The route we're on now is actually a chain of letterboxes, each one containing clues on how to find the next box. This route has taken us along the south rim of Cottonwood Canyon and some of its side canyons. Beautiful country. We've been following this chain all day and we're still not done. We'll come back another day to finish it. It's a ten letterbox chain and we've only found the first seven so far."

Rivera was intrigued. As the four continued to talk about their quest, he learned they were all students at the University of Colorado in Boulder and they'd started letterboxing about two years ago. They'd done about a dozen searches in Colorado and Utah since then. They wrote down for him the name of a website that contained letterboxing clues and starting points. One of the young men mentioned there was also a high-tech version of letterboxing called geo-caching where a GPS receiver is used to locate the boxes and the internet clues are provided in latitude and longitude coordinates.

"Well, it's getting late," said the blonde. "We need to get back to our vehicle while there's still daylight." They said goodbye and departed, the sounds of their voices and laughter fading into the distance.

Rivera was alone again. He reflected on the adventure the young people were undertaking. Then he remembered the bikers who'd found the body yesterday and the camaraderie that they, too, shared as they met the challenge of conquering the Kokopelli trail. He envied them all and made a vow: *I'm going to start enjoying this beautiful country more, just as soon as the pressures of this case are over.*

He got into his vehicle and drove across Fisher Valley until he reached the winding dirt road that

descended to Onion Creek and followed its meanders. The water-filled potholes of yesterday were now
mostly dry. As he drove, he studied the beautiful mini-
canyon that Onion Creek had cut into the sandstone.
The color of the shallow canyon walls changed from
reddish-purple to greenish-grey to tan-ochre and back
to reddish purple. He'd tried one time to explain the
colorful geology of the Moab area to his grandmother
in Las Cruces, but could never find the words to convey
the picture. Even photographs had proven incapable of
doing the job. You just had to see it for yourself. Finally,
he reached the pavement of Highway 128 and headed
toward Moab. The sun had dropped behind the Moab
Rim by the time he arrived back at his office.

7

MILLIE IVES LOOKED up from her dispatcher's workstation as Rivera came through the door.

"Sheriff wants to see you Manny," she said, looking over her granny glasses. She lowered her voice, "He's a bit tense today."

Rivera nodded, thanked her, and went to his office. He closed the door and fell heavily into his chair, disappointed that his Kokopelli Trail search had proven fruitless. He reached into his in-box and extracted the two reports it contained. The first was from the FBI, a reply to his query regarding Montoya's fingerprints. Their databases had produced no match. The second, a report from the Texas Department of Public Safety, indicated that upon expanding their search, four driver's licenses with the name Jesse B. Montoya had been issued or renewed in south Texas during the past ten years. The current ages of the men were 83, 61, 46, and 25. The only possibility would be the 25-year old, but Rivera ruled him out as he was currently serving with the U.S. Navy in Bahrain.

He ran a check on the Rutherford Ranch personnel, including Mr. Rutherford himself, for wants and
warrants. The results from the FBI and the Utah State
Police databases came back negative. No reason to believe anyone at the ranch was involved in the killing.
He walked down the hallway to the sheriff's office,
knocked, and entered. Sheriff Bradshaw looked up. His
expression revealed great interest and great concern.
Rivera updated him on everything he'd learned during
the day. Which was very little. At the end of the briefing,
the men sat looking at each other, both recognizing
the investigation had come up empty thus far.

"Nothing much to grab onto," said Rivera.

"No, but keep digging," said Bradshaw. He paused
for a moment, leaned forward, and spoke in a soft voice.
"A lot of investigations begin this way, Manny. In most
cases, persistence and attention to detail pay off more
than clever detective work. Progress usually comes in
small steps rather than one big breakthrough."

Rivera nodded, appreciating the encouragement
he'd received instead of the criticism he'd anticipated.

The sheriff continued, "The business owners in
town are troubled by all this. So are our politicians.
You can appreciate their point of view. The whole
community is buzzing. The *Times-Independent* weekly
newspaper is due out tomorrow morning with a front
page story on Montoya's killing. They were all over us
during the day asking for details on our progress and

questioning whether hikers are safe in the backcountry. And the *Salt Lake Tribune* ran a short page-three story today with the headline *Killer in the Canyon Country*." Bradshaw paused, picked up a sheet of paper from his desk and scanned it. "This month alone, we've got the Jeep Jamboree, the 24-Hours of Moab Bike Race, the Half-Marathon, the Moab Century Bike Tour, and the Rumble in the Red Rocks. Several art and music functions are also scheduled. Thousands of tourists. I can understand why my phone's been ringing off the hook for the past two days. But that's my problem and I'll take care of it. Your job is to concentrate one-hundred percent on this. Follow all leads, no matter how insignificant they seem. And if you need help, tell me right away." The sheriff got up, signaling the meeting was over. Both men walked toward the door. Bradshaw put his hand on his deputy's shoulder. "Just keep pushing on this, Manny."

"Yes Sir," said Rivera, wondering if he was in over his head.

After finishing up the work on his desk, Rivera left the office and went home. He slid a frozen pizza into the oven, set the temperature at 400 degrees, and opened a can of beer. He took a long, refreshing swallow, and turned toward the aquarium. As usual, the guppies were crowded into the corner of the tank, dancing and darting like they always did, trying to get his attention. He dropped in a pinch of food, and lingered awhile as the guppies ate. Watching the fish usually relaxed him, allowed him to enter another world, a calm and beautiful one, devoid of schedules and pressure. But not tonight. He couldn't stop thinking about his case. What would his next step be? He spent the next hour eating pizza, drinking beer, and trying to watch a *Rockford Files* rerun on the small TV in his kitchen. But his mind kept coming back to Jesse Montoya and Sheriff Bradshaw, and, of course, his own lack of progress. He had a vague sense of time running out. Meanwhile, on TV, Jim Rockford was solving his case with flair and flourish. Disgusted, Rivera got up and shut off the TV.

He folded the pizza box in half and stuffed it into the kitchen trash can. As he wiped off the kitchen table, his mother's home-cooking entered his thoughts. He missed it. And his grandmother's enchiladas were his favorite meal. The fast food which had become a staple of his life couldn't compare. He'd bought a cookbook last year, but never got around to using it. It rested on the kitchen countertop, still unopened. He wondered when he'd be able to get a few days off for a drive down to Las Cruces to see his family. Probably not any time soon. His mind was suddenly filled with memories of home, his three sisters and two brothers, and his many cousins and friends. And here he was, sitting around in an empty house, feeling like a failure, alone. All things considered, this had not been a good day for Manuel Rivera.

He showered, climbed into bed, and tried reading a novel Millie had loaned him a week ago. "You'll love it," she'd said as she pressed it into his hand. But he couldn't make it past page three. He dropped the book on the nightstand, set the alarm, and turned off the bedside lamp. His body was tired but his mind was still racing, so he just lay there, hands clasped behind his head, staring into the darkness. His introspection resumed. He needed a more balanced life, less work and worry, more fun time with friends. He thought back to the three bikers as they had ridden away from the crime scene, pursuing their quest to ride their mountain bikes from one end of the Kokopelli trail to the other. Friends sharing a challenging journey across the backcountry. And the two couples he'd met today letterboxing their way around the LaSal Mountains seemed to be enjoying life to the fullest. He tried to form a mental picture of what letterboxing would be like. Following the clues with friends on a beautiful day, searching for the next box in the chain, the excitement of finding it, and then adding his name to the list of previous treasure hunters. It was at that moment the idea struck him.

He sat up, swung his legs over the side of the bed, and turned on the lamp. There was still another possibility he could explore. Tomorrow, he would return to the crime scene and pick up the trail of the letterboxes along the rim of Cottonwood Canyon. Maybe the boxes contained names entered on the date of the crime. It was a long shot, but if hikers had been in the vicinity that day, perhaps someone had seen something that would be useful. He would check the letterbox website in the morning, find the starting point, and then go letterboxing.

As the sheriff had said, progress usually comes in small steps. And this would be Rivera's next step. He turned off the light, swung back into bed, and fell sound asleep.

8

FRANK SORENSON'S HEART was pounding as two
Sheriff's Department vehicles chased him up Highway
128. As he sped around a curve in the road, he saw the
roadblock up ahead. Uniformed officers were standing
behind their vehicles, weapons drawn. He jammed on
his brakes and skidded to a halt, his vehicle spinning
completely around. The two chase vehicles were upon
him, red lights flashing and sirens wailing. He woke up
with a jolt, drenched with sweat, the sirens transforming
themselves into the buzzing clock radio in his Moab
motel room. Shaken, he shut off the alarm and sat up,
still feeling the residual effects of fear. As the sensation
faded, he realized he'd been having trouble sleeping
the past few nights, a problem he'd never had before.
Was it caused by the pressure of retrieving and selling
the Indian artifacts or his feelings of guilt for having
shot that ranch hand? Or both? He got up, took a long
cold shower, and got dressed. Slowly, he began to feel
normal again.

He'd spent yesterday back in Salt Lake City resting and reviewing his plan, evaluating the potential effect of the killing on his procedures. He'd been visiting the cave twice a week since he'd begun selling the pots and figurines. But now, with law enforcement officers presumably investigating the area around Cottonwood and Burro Canyons, he wondered if he should wait before resuming his operation, not just a few days, but a few weeks or even longer. His intellect was flashing a caution signal. But his gut and his Special Forces training told him to get more aggressive and bold even in the face of increased danger. Finish the mission. Sell the pots and figurines in the cave as fast as Twitchell can find buyers for them. After all, this would likely be the only chance in his lifetime to become wealthy. Finally he decided: he would step up his activities, trusting that his "lost hiker" cover story would hold up should he encounter a cop in the canyons.

Sorenson had called Twitchell yesterday afternoon. He told him he could deliver three items on each of the following three days. Same place, 2:00 P.M. each day, three days straight. Twitchell said he'd been very successful lately in finding buyers and could take nine items, even more if they were available. He gave Sorenson nine item numbers from the master list which corresponded to seven pots and two figurines. Twitchell asked if he could just get all nine artifacts on a single trip to save all that driving between Farmington and

Cedar Mesa. "After all, I'm an old man," he'd said with a forced laugh. Sorenson said no, he wanted to keep the procedure just as it had been, three pieces at a time. He didn't reveal his rationale for delivering only three per trip, that if something went wrong or Twitchell double-crossed him, he would only lose three items. The artifact trader had sighed loudly and acquiesced. Three each day it would be.

After topping off his fuel tank, Sorenson went to the grocery store to buy supplies for the three days he would be in Moab. His motel room had a small refrigerator and a microwave so he'd be able to eat breakfast and dinner there, generally staying out of sight to reduce the chances of someone recognizing him, wondering what he was doing in Moab, becoming inquisitive. He'd eat snack bars and fruit on the trail. After picking up the items on his grocery list, he proceeded to the checkout line. There he saw a stack of *Times-Independent* newspapers for sale. Muscles tightened in the pit of his stomach when he saw the headline:

SEARCH FOR BACKCOUNTRY KILLER CONTINUES

He picked up a copy and added it to his groceries.

Back in his motel room, he stored the perishables in the refrigerator and sat down on the bed. He picked up the newspaper and began reading. The man he'd killed now had an identity: Jesse B. Montoya. For some reason, knowing the victim's name increased Sorenson's feelings of guilt. His appetite for breakfast left him. He sat there for a moment, staring at the floor, feeling a numbness of spirit.

He got up from the bed and walked to the window. It was still early so the traffic on Main Street was light. A lone runner jogged past. Sorenson thought about the sequence of events that had led him to this point in life. If he had it to do all over again, would he? An uncomfortable question. After thinking about it, he finally admitted to himself that he would. It was the powerful combination of opportunity and greed that had produced that newspaper headline.

He read through the rest of the article. The man was a recently-hired ranch hand at the Rutherford Ranch. He was just doing his job, scouting the canyons on the west end of the ranch for strays. The article included quotations attributed to some of the local politicians. One of their concerns was the potential impact of the crime on tourism. They'd stated that solving this crime was "priority one" and they had every confidence the sheriff would apprehend the killer soon. The story was pretty much what Sorenson would have expected, except that the newspaper had gotten the location of the crime scene wrong. The article stated Montoya's body had been found at the head of Cottonwood Canyon near the Kokopelli Trail, miles from Burro Canyon.

He wondered about that, finally concluding the sheriff had deliberately issued incorrect information in order to keep the curious from tromping around the actual crime-scene area.

Sorenson dropped the newspaper to the floor, sat back, and began reflecting on the events that had changed his life. If only his and Montoya's paths hadn't crossed on that fateful day, things would be different. But they did cross and no amount of regret would ever change what happened.

The newspaper article on the killing caused him to rethink his plan. Was he taking too big a chance? He reviewed his procedures, thinking everything through, step by step. In the end, he decided the newspaper article itself hadn't really changed anything. Nor did it provide any new information. It underscored the risk he was taking but didn't alter it in any way. Back in his Army days, he was used to flirting with extreme danger. Even thrived on it. As a sniper, he'd taken on many perilous assignments and handled them with courage and precision. Those instincts still resided somewhere within him. Caution, patience, and preparation usually overcame what others perceived to be excessive risk. But as he analyzed his procedures, he recognized one step that could be improved.

The riskiest part of the operation was removing the pots from the cave and carrying them one-at-a-time down the talus to his backpack. This had been the best way to minimize the risk of damaging the merchandise, but it left the pots visually exposed. Indeed, that's what he'd been doing when Montoya caught him red handed. He decided to make one modification to his procedure: He would carry the backpack up into the cave, fill it with three items in the privacy of the cave and then depart. The new risk was that the backpack would cause his descent down the talus to become more precarious. An errant step could destroy three pots instead of just one. But it was feasible. And this modification to the plan would have two positive effects. First, the pots would never be within sight of someone who happened to be in the area. And second, he would be wearing a backpack at all times while outside the cave so that, if seen, he could always use the standard excuse that he was a hiker who'd simply gotten lost. The new plan seemed logical and safe.

There was, of course, another alternative. He could simply disappear from the Moab area for an extended period, perhaps a few months. The investigation would likely have cooled off by then. But leaving valuable items in the cave for that much longer was risky. Anything could happen. Maybe someone else would find them. The pots were his and he didn't want to take that chance. He decided to continue retrieving and selling the pots as fast as possible, and be prepared to convincingly use his "lost hiker" cover story. All things considered, finishing the mission in the shortest possible time seemed like the wisest course of action.

He left his motel room carrying a sack of snack bars, apples, and bottled water, and headed for his truck. The weather man on TV had predicted a cold front would arrive in the afternoon, so he also brought along a sweat shirt and a windbreaker. He got into the truck, closed the door, and reached under the seat to verify that his revolver was still in place. He would continue to carry a handgun on each hike down the canyon. He hoped to God he would never have to use it again, but discovery of the cave by another person was not acceptable. He started the engine, pulled out of the motel parking lot, and drove north out of Moab, turning right on Highway 128.

Sorenson followed his usual route, driving upriver to the Castle Valley cutoff, through Castle Valley to the foothills of the LaSal Mountains, then left on the gravel Castleton-Gateway Road, and left again on the rocky dirt road called the Thompson Canyon Trail. After a short bumpy drive, he pulled off the road and parked his pickup behind a thicket of junipers. He opened the glove compartment, retrieved the two-page list of artifacts he kept there, and placed it on the seat next to him. From his shirt pocket he pulled out a sheet of paper and unfolded it. It contained the notes he'd made during his last conversation with Twitchell.

The trader wanted pots #16, #19, and #51 delivered to him today. Sorenson reached into the glove compartment, removed a stack of photographs held together with a rubber band, and thumbed through them. He removed the photos of the three artifacts and studied them. The first was a 700-year old twelve-inch Gila polychrome bowl with black and white geometric patterns. The second was a ten-inch Salado redware pot with a smoothed-over corrugated finish. The third was his favorite, a large 19th century Zuni olla with a square-winged rainbird design. He stared at it. For a fleeting moment, he felt a sense of loss in having to part with it.

He stuffed the three photographs into his shirt pocket and got out of the truck. He strapped on his special backpack, secured his revolver in the holster under his shirt, and trekked over to Cottonwood Canyon.

Once in the canyon, he made the long hike down to Burro Canyon and up the steep slope to the cave. Inside, he retrieved the three pots, carefully comparing each to its corresponding photograph to ensure he was bringing the right merchandise to the rendezvous scheduled for later that day. He wrapped each one and gently placed it into his backpack. The cash for today would total $41,200. Pure profit and tax-free. During the hike back to his truck, he saw no one. He left the area the usual way, driving on the gravel roads that wrapped around the east side of the mountains, and from there onto the pavement of Highway 46. He drove through Blanding to the Cedar Mesa exchange point where he placed the cardboard box behind the designated rock at the rendezvous point. Then he made the long circuitous drive to his overlook on the bluff. By the time he got there, the wind began kicking up and the temperature started dropping fast. The expected cold front had arrived. He put on his extra clothing, walked to the edge of the bluff, and sat down.

Sometime later, Twitchell's Rubicon appeared on the horizon. The exchange went perfectly as it always had, and the money was exactly right. Sorenson locked the paper bag containing the cash in the toolbox welded behind the cab of his truck. Then he followed the dirt roads back to the pavement and returned to Moab. It was dark by the time he pulled into the motel parking lot.

Knowing he had to repeat this same strenuous sequence for each of the next two days, he ate, watched a little TV, and went to bed early with his alarm set for 6:00 A.M.

As Sorenson lay there in the darkness, he mentally tallied up the cash he would have after selling all the items in the cave. It would come to well over a half-million dollars, more money than he'd ever dreamed would be his.

9

DONALD TWITCHELL SAT in his favorite stuffed chair in front of the fireplace, his feet resting on a matching ottoman. Flames rose from the crackling pinyon logs. He was generally pleased with himself.

His new business venture was producing substantial profits, and there was much more to come, judging by the stack of artifact photos his supplier had given him. He'd been involved in questionable business enterprises like this before, but never one so intriguing and certainly never one on this scale. But where were all the artifacts coming from? With each new delivery, his curiosity rose another notch. There were too many for the seller to have found them *in situ*. And the quality of the merchandise was exceptional. Possibly they'd been stolen from a museum or a private collection, but he wasn't aware of any theft in the antiquities world that would explain what was taking place.

Staring at the flames, he raised his glass to his lips and took a sip of twelve-year-old single malt scotch. He always enjoyed the way the first sip thoroughly warmed his insides. Perhaps the artifacts had been stolen from a collection but the owner hadn't yet realized they were missing. But that wasn't likely. It might be possible for one or two missing pieces to go unnoticed, but not several dozen. At retail, the whole lot was worth over a million dollars. Serious collectors guarded their collections like gold ingots.

A loud pop in the fireplace produced a small shower of sparks. So where were these treasures coming from? He smiled, a part of him enjoying the mystery of it all. He took another sip. If the artifacts weren't stolen, then why all this secrecy about the seller's identity? If the seller owned the artifacts legally, he would have come through the front door of the store and negotiated the deal face-to-face. Or he would have commissioned Sotheby's or Christie's to auction them off and made even more than he's making with the current arrangement.

On the telephone, the seller had seemed intelligent, organized, and resolute. He'd cleverly set up the business deal without ever revealing his identity. Twitchell knew he'd been hooked by the vast quantity of artifacts which represented an enormous profit. He'd also been hooked by the first pot—the gift, the sign of good faith—that the seller had given him. It was one of the lesser pieces with a retail value of about five thousand dollars. But it had established the seller as a serious business partner. Twitchell had to admit he was impressed with the seller. But he knew he wasn't an expert in artifacts. He'd already incorrectly priced a rare polychrome pot that was worth four or five times what he'd asked for it.

Twitchell pushed himself out of his chair and shuffled over to the fireplace. He used a wrought iron poker to maneuver a half-burned log back into the flames. He stood there for a couple of minutes, leaning against the mantel, allowing the warmth of the fire to soak into his arthritic joints. One thing that puzzled him was why the seller insisted on selling only three items at a time. He returned to his chair and sat down. Took another sip. He stared at the fire and resumed his analysis of the mysterious deal he'd become part of. It was possible the seller was coming into possession of the artifacts only three at a time. Could the seller then be just a middle-man? If so, who was his supplier? Twitchell felt a mild sense of frustration building within him. The questions were piling up without answers. He was the artifact master, the guru, and yet he was unable to make any sense of what was going on. Sure, it was profitable, but that wasn't the point. He already had more money than he could ever spend. It was acute curiosity and not money that was driving his thoughts. The seller had Twitchell at a disadvantage. He knew Twitchell's identity but Twitchell was left in the dark. That didn't sit well with him. He began to feel bested, bested by an amateur in the world of Indian artifacts. His curiosity was slowly giving way to a strong competitive sense. Here's some damn upstart doing something so clever that it's driving the old master to the edge of frustration. The setup was both intriguing and irritating, and Twitchell couldn't stop tumbling it around in his mind. He thought again about the man on the phone. He seemed politely cocky, a confident man who probably went through life being quite sure of himself. Maybe he should be taught a lesson by Donald A. Twitchell, a master in such matters.

It wouldn't be too difficult to have someone arrive very early at Cedar Mesa up on top of the bluff, say a half-mile from his supplier's perch, and watch the transaction take place. The supplier, when he departed with the money, could then be followed to see where he lived and ultimately who he was. Then, eventually, he could be followed to his source. Not too difficult at all. He thought of Biggs or Miggs or whatever that guy's name was. He was an investigator who worked for attorneys or suspicious spouses or anyone with money who wanted someone followed and photographed. And he had the reputation of being an experienced backcountry tracker. He was relatively new to the area, but had quickly developed an excellent track record.

That was certainly a way to satisfy Twitchell's curiosity about what was going on. Of course, he would never consider cutting out his supplier—Twitchell wasn't a welsher. And besides, a double cross could be dangerous. The seller knew right where to find him. In any case, Twitchell would rigorously adhere to the terms of their business deal. But satisfying his curiosity—that was a different matter.

Twitchell lifted his glass, tilted back his head, and let the last of the single malt slide down his throat. He smiled at himself and shook his head. Perhaps putting a tail on his supplier wasn't such a good idea. Things were going well and he was making a killing. Maybe he shouldn't risk screwing everything up.

It was getting late and he was tired. He would think about it some more in the morning.

10

A GUST OF cold morning air bounced a tumbleweed down Main Street as a hungry Manny Rivera turned his Sheriff's Department pickup into the parking lot next to the Rim Rock Diner. He walked to the front door, opened it, and stepped into the warmth. The smell of pancakes and bacon greeted him, as did the sounds of friendly conversation and the clinking of utensils against plates. For Rivera, the diner had a comfortable familiarity. He loved starting his day here. It was the closest thing he had to a real home in Moab. At the counter were the three Benson brothers, local craftsmen who were helping to build the new condos out in Spanish Valley. They were eating breakfast and discussing the rising prices of Moab real estate. They smiled and waved at Rivera as he passed them. Four grizzled old-timers sat in their usual booth discussing the merits of nuclear power and making projections on the price of uranium and when the mines would finally reopen. The discourse was lively and the men were obviously enjoying each other's company. Rivera exchanged greetings with them as he walked toward his regular booth next to the window in the far corner.

On the walls of the diner hung dozens of framed black-and-white photographs of old Moab. Rivera hardly noticed them now, but when he first entered the diner as a brand new deputy, he looked at each one closely, studying them and digesting the history of the area in pictures. Photos of the town in the 1950s, during Moab's uranium boom, showed the old storefronts on Main Street, men on horseback, and the vintage automobiles and pickup trucks of that era. Other photos showed mine entrances with men and machinery at work. Still others showed the old uranium mill and the tailings of processed ore. Since then, Moab had evolved from a typical old west mining town into an outdoor recreation paradise. Rivera genuinely liked Moab and its people. Although he missed his family, he was glad he'd decided to relocate here.

He slid into the booth and looked out the window at Main Street. For some reason, it reminded him of one of his first assignments as a deputy, that of informing Old Lady Donegan it would be better if she rode her motorized wheelchair on the sidewalk instead of down the middle of the street. He smiled as he replayed the memory. He politely explained to her that the drivers of pickup trucks and SUVs were up high and might not be able to see her down so low in her wheelchair. She pointed out that the wheelchair was equipped with a tall staff on which flew a bright pink flag that was high enough for the drivers to see. Even so, he'd said, the wheelchair was not licensed as a road vehicle. And besides, the sidewalks were wheelchair friendly, each corner having ramps to accommodate the handicapped. He could still see her, with white hair and skin like wrinkled leather, nodding in agreement and grinning her toothless smile. The next day, he saw her again, motoring smartly down the middle of Main Street, this time flying a black flag with a white skull-and-crossbones. He mentioned this to his colleagues back at the sheriff's office and they all howled with laughter. Whenever she flew the Jolly Roger, they told him, everyone knew to back off or they'd get a good ear-chewing. Rivera learned that all new deputies were assigned the job of correcting Old Lady Donegan's bad driving habits, but no one had yet succeeded. It was a rite of passage for rookie cops.

Betty approached his table with a mug and a pot of coffee.

"Mornin' handsome," she said, smiling at him with a big grin and slowly chewing her gum. Her bleached blond hair was done up in something between a French twist and a beehive, and her white uniform was one size too small. She filled his coffee mug.

"Good morning, Betty. Emmett will be joining me shortly."

"Good. I like seeing young hunks all dressed up in their tan uniforms. Makes me feel real warm and safe." Her grin broadened and she continued staring at him. He smiled back, hoping he wasn't blushing.

After Mitchell had arrived and both deputies had ordered ham, eggs, hash browns, and wheat toast, they settled into a discussion about the tourists in town and their expensive off-road vehicles. Mitchell was telling Rivera about a man in his twenties who was driving a custom four-wheel drive with a jacked-up suspension, huge tires, a custom transmission, and advanced communications and navigation gear. The rig was probably worth $150,000. It seems the fellow tried to drive up into the arch at Looking Glass Rock but the vehicle rolled over backwards and bounced down the sandstone. The driver was uninjured but the vehicle was badly damaged. The fellow was smiling about the whole thing, seemingly unconcerned about the repair bill that awaited him. Rivera was interested but wanted to change the subject. He wanted to ask Mitchell what he thought about the letterboxing idea. He waited until his friend had finished his story and then began telling him about his progress to date on the Montoya case. Or lack of it. Then he mentioned his idea of letterboxing for clues. Mitchell smiled. As Rivera detailed the plan, Mitchell's smile expanded into a grin.

"You're gonna go letterboxing in the middle of a high profile murder case?"

Deflated, Rivera sat back. "I know it's a long shot, but I have no leads. Nothing. I've got to develop something. And quick."

Mitchell's grin broadened. "Boy, you Grand County deputies sure have the life. Why, down in San Juan County, getting paid for letterboxing is a concept our county commissioners have yet to cozy up to. We servants of the people to the south of your great county have to *work* all day long to justify our paychecks."

Rivera leaned forward and lowered his voice to a whisper. "Really, Emmett, I'm kind of desperate."

Mitchell laughed a friendly laugh. "My brother and I did some letterboxing on Cedar Mesa many years ago. It's actually a lot of fun. You'll enjoy it."

"Well, the truth is I'm kind of looking forward to it. I've never done it before."

"Well, try not to enjoy it *too* much."

Back at the office, Rivera accessed the letterboxing website. After a few minutes of searching, he found the starting place for the series of ten boxes he was interested in, and printed out the directions to the first box.

He hurried out of the office, hopped into his pickup, and drove out of town and upriver on Highway 128. Twenty-one miles later, he turned right on Onion Creek Road and pulled over. He unfolded the printed instructions and reread them. After the third creek crossing, he was to proceed one hundred feet where he would see a small wash to his right. About fifteen feet up the wash, on the left, he would see a hole in the face of the bluff about chest high. *Reach in and remove the rock that protects the letterbox*, the instructions said. He resumed driving, following the meanders of Onion Creek until he crossed it a third time. He stopped his truck and shut off the engine. He walked up the wash and located the hole. After inspecting it for the presence of desert creatures that bite, he removed the rock and the old cookie tin hidden behind it. He popped off the lid. Inside he found a small spiral notepad and a rubber stamp. He set those aside. He extracted the printed instructions which had been laminated in clear plastic. As expected, they provided the clues to finding the next box in the series. Rivera smiled, enjoying the moment. He'd found his first letterbox. He began to understand why the young people he'd met yesterday were having such a good time. Then he remembered Mitchell's words about not having too much fun and chuckled to himself.

He wrote down the instructions for locating Box #2 in his pocket notebook. Then, consulting the spiral notepad, he was encouraged to see that several people had visited Box #1 on October 4th, the day of the crime. He entered their names into his notebook:

DATE	NAME	FROM	COMMENTS
Oct 4	Randy Jackson	Flagstaff AZ	Started at 6:22 AM
Oct 4	Joe & Sue Phillips	Salt Lake City	Beautiful morning!
Oct 4	Martin Anderson +3	Provo	Here we go!
Oct 4	Daniel Tsopoulis	Farmington	Nice country
Oct 4	The Parkers	Monticello	ThanksLord!

The thought of adding his own name to the list crossed his mind but he resisted the urge. After all, this *was* supposed to be work. He looked at the rubber stamp before he dropped it back into the box. It appeared to be the image of a smiling lizard. He inserted the spiral notepad and the laminated instructions back into the container and secured the lid. Then he placed the box and the rock back into the hole.

Back in his vehicle, he reread the instructions for finding Box #2:

> *Hike upstream to where the road leaves Onion Creek and ascends to Fisher Valley. At the top of the winding road, walk fifty yards east to a grey rock that looks like a large Buddha. Just behind that rock, find a flat piece of grey shale lying on the ground. Box #2 is hidden underneath.*

Because he was driving the route instead of hiking it, Rivera felt a bit guilty. Weren't *real* letterboxers supposed to *hike* the trail? Nevertheless, he followed the instructions and soon discovered Box #2. He opened it and reviewed the contents, glad to see that all the hikers had made it this far. He wrote down the instructions for locating Box #3. There was also a set of instructions for finding Box #1. This puzzled him for a moment until he recalled reading on the web site that hikers could choose to follow the chain of letterboxes in reverse direction, starting at Box #10 and finishing at Box #1. He went in search of Box #3 and arrived at a point near the intersection of the Kokopelli Trail and Cottonwood Canyon, the place where he'd seen the four young letterboxers yesterday, and close to the spot where Montoya's body had been found. The instructions directed him to proceed to the back side of a two-hundred-foot-high hillock covered with sagebrush, yucca, and rocks. The letterbox was located sixty feet east of the large grayish-green boulder at the base. No problem. He easily found Box #3. The list of names showed that all the hikers had continued to this point. He read the instructions for locating Box #4:

> *Proceed 5.3 miles up the rocky Kokopelli Trail towards Thompson Canyon. There you will find a large dead cottonwood tree. Proceed to*

*a point 100 feet northwest of the tree. Find a
single fencepost with a roll of rusted barbed
wire hanging on it. A rock at the base of the
fencepost covers Box #4.*

The deputy followed the instructions, and after
several minutes of searching for the right tree, found
Box #4. He began thinking how well his day was going.
He was making good time. His goal was to examine all
the boxes along Cottonwood Canyon and return by late
afternoon. He reviewed the list of names for October
4th inside Box #4:

DATE	NAME	FROM	COMMENTS
Oct 4	Randy Jackson	Flag.	
Oct 4	Joe and Sue Phillips	SLC	Enjoyed it!
Oct 4	Martin Anderson +3	Provo	Getting tired
Oct 4	The Parkers	Monticello	Great hike
Oct 4	Andy Blinn	Moab	Done for the day

The last name seemed familiar to him. He had a
vague recollection of having met Andy Blinn in Moab
sometime in the past. Blinn must have started at Box
#10 and hiked the chain of boxes in reverse order,
terminating his hike at Box #4. And Daniel Tsopoulis
must have decided to end his hike after Box #3. The
instructions for finding Box #5 were a bit ominous:

This is the point where the hiking gets difficult. Be sure to bring water, food, a compass, and a good map. Proceed northeast for 1.4 miles to the place where Thompson Canyon connects with Cottonwood Canyon. Near the far tip of the mesa, there are two juniper trees. Box #5 is hidden under a small pile of rocks midway between them.

Rivera realized he'd been on the easy end of the chain and his travel was about to become more challenging. He consulted his map and saw it would be impossible to continue the trip in his vehicle. The terrain was simply too rough. He parked in a clearing by the side of the road and continued on foot toward the northeast. Since there was no apparent trail, he found himself continually pushing aside brush and juniper branches, stepping over rocks, avoiding cactus, and stumbling across endless arroyos. He checked his compass heading frequently since the process of obstacle avoidance made traveling in a straight line impossible, and maintaining one's sense of direction was problematic.

In a clearing, he came upon a jackrabbit that stared at him with wide-eyed curiosity and then scampered off into the dense brush. Finally, after an hour of difficult hiking, he arrived at the junction of the two canyons. As promised, there was a box located under a pile of rocks between the two junipers. Before opening it, he took a moment to sit down, relax, and massage his calves. The red rock canyons below him were extraordinary. He wondered how many human beings had ever been in this exact place. Probably not many. He took a drink of water from the plastic bottle he carried with him. He looked at the level of water remaining in the bottle. It was getting low and he realized he should have brought more. He reached over, picked up the box, and opened it. He recorded the names in his notebook:

DATE	NAME	FROM	COMMENTS
Oct 4	Randy Jackson	Flag.	
Oct 4	The Parkers	Monticello	Heaven!
Oct 4	Andy Blinn	Moab	Extraordinary

The Phillips couple and the Anderson group had not made it this far. Apparently pushing through the brush wasn't for them. Considering the many scratches on his hands and wrists, he could understand why. He wrote down the directions for finding Box #6 and pressed on. It was located to the south about 1.6 miles, in upper Thompson Canyon. A large rock cairn would mark the spot. He consulted his map and realized that more hiking over rough terrain was in store. An hour later, after an extensive search, he found Box #6. It yielded the following names:

DATE	NAME	FROM	COMMENTS
Oct 4	Randy Jackson	Flag.	
Oct 4	Andy Blinn	Moab	Great route

Rivera recorded the names. The Parkers had dropped out after Box #5. Jackson had continued, traveling in the same direction as Rivera. Blinn had been traveling in the opposite direction.

The directions for Box #7 took him across the head of Thompson Canyon and then north to a place near where Burro Canyon joined Cottonwood Canyon. Again, the hike was strenuous, but Rivera arrived at the correct spot late in the afternoon and found the box. The names in Box #7 were identical to those in Box #6.

From there the instructions for finding Box #8 led south about four miles along the west rim of Burro Canyon and out of Rivera's area of interest. Consequently, he terminated the letterboxing journey, drank the last of his water, and began the long hike back to his vehicle. He'd gotten what he came for. Now he could only hope that the people whose names he'd collected had seen something useful that day.

11

IT WAS EVENING by the time Rivera arrived back at the office. He began the task of tracking down home phone numbers. He found listings for everyone except Randy Jackson. He called Andy Blinn of Moab first, got reacquainted with him, and told him he was calling all letterboxers who were in the vicinity of Cottonwood Canyon on October 4th to see if they'd seen anyone or anything unusual out there that day. Blinn stated that he'd hiked the letterbox chain in reverse, making it as far as Box #4. He'd only seen one other person, another letterboxer traveling in the opposite direction. He estimated that it was mid-afternoon and he couldn't recall the guy's name, but did remember that he was a student from Flagstaff. Other than that he'd seen nothing out of the ordinary. Rivera thanked him and hung up.

He called the Parkers in Monticello next. Mrs. Parker answered. She and her husband had read about the murder in the newspaper and were shocked and frightened when they realized they were in the same vicinity as the killer on the day of the murder. But they'd neither seen nor heard anything unusual. She added that they loved hiking the backcountry around Moab but would be very reluctant to return until the killer was apprehended. The conversation reminded him of what the sheriff had said about tourism and the importance of solving this crime quickly. The palpable fear in Mrs. Parker's voice had underscored the urgency of his assignment.

He talked to the Phillips couple, then Martin Anderson, and finally, Daniel Tsopoulis. None of them had seen anything out of the ordinary. Feelings of frustration began seeping into Rivera's consciousness. Randy Jackson was now his only hope. But there was no Randy Jackson listed in the Flagstaff telephone directory. He called the Flagstaff Police Department to see if they had any information on Jackson. Unfortunately, they did not. Rivera sat there, considering what he would do next. Had he wasted an entire day? Then he recalled that Andy Blinn had said the guy he'd met on the trail was a student. He called Northern Arizona University in Flagstaff, identified himself, and asked if they had a student by the name of Randy Jackson enrolled. They did and ten minutes later he had Jackson on the phone.

"Why do the police want to talk to *me*?" said the young man in a nervous voice. Rivera assured him he was in no trouble. He said he was seeking information that might be related to a homicide which took place in Cottonwood Canyon on October 4th.

"You were out there letterboxing that day. Did you see anything unusual while you were hiking, anything at all?"

Jackson's voice now sounded relaxed. "Not really. Everything seemed pretty normal. Beautiful country. Friends of mine at school had told me about that particular chain of letterboxes. They said it was a great hike and the chain was well laid out and the boxes well maintained. There's a group of us here at NAU who are into letterboxing big-time. Anyway, I decided to do it alone. Kind of like a spiritual retreat. You know, solitude and getting close to nature and all that. I did the whole chain from Box #1 to Box #10 in one day. One *long* day." He paused, then added, "I remember seeing only one other person out there. Another letterboxer. The guy said he was from Moab."

"You mean Andy Blinn," said Rivera.

"Yeah, that was his name. Nice fellow. He was heading … Hey, wait a minute, I almost forgot. I also saw a couple of guys and a pickup truck down below in the canyon. From where I was standing when I saw them, they were about a hundred yards down-canyon from me. I was on the rim several hundred feet above them, so I didn't get a real good look at them."

"What were they doing?"

"I think one of them must have been injured. The big guy was helping the smaller fellow back to the pickup truck. When they got there, he lifted him up and put him in the passenger-side seat. After that, the big one went back and retrieved the other guy's hat which was on the ground. Then he returned to the truck and they drove off. And that's all I saw."

"How big was the big one?'

"Looked like a big strapping guy. I'd guess over six feet. Wore a dark cowboy hat. At that distance, I couldn't tell you much else about him."

"And the smaller man?"

"I'd say around five foot seven, maybe 150 pounds, maybe less."

"What color was the truck?"

"It was pretty dirty, but I'd say it was a light color. Maybe a light tan or grey. It was one of those extended-cab pickups with four doors."

Rivera wrote Jackson's comments verbatim into his notepad.

"Which way did the truck go when it drove off?"

"It went toward Cottonwood Canyon."

"*Toward* Cottonwood Canyon?" asked Rivera, surprised. "I thought you meant they were *in* Cottonwood Canyon. Where exactly did you see them?"

"They were in Burro Canyon, a short way up from where it connects to Cottonwood Canyon. I was at the letterbox that's near the junction of the two canyons. I don't recall the box number."

Rivera remembered the spot. Looking at his notes, he saw that it was Box #7.

"Tell me as best you can *exactly* where they were in Burro Canyon when you saw them," he said.

"I'd say they were between fifty and a hundred yards up into Burro Canyon from where it joins Cottonwood." Jackson paused, as if trying to picture the scene. "As I remember it, when I first saw them, they were near a large rock, a rectangular-shaped piece of cap rock about the size of an automobile, on the west side of the canyon floor. A whitish-grey rock. Bigger than the other rocks down there. The truck was parked back closer to the main canyon."

"Anything else you can remember?"

"No, that's pretty much everything."

"Call me back if you remember anything else. It's very important," said Rivera. He gave Jackson his phone number, thanked him, and hung up.

Rivera leaned back in his chair. Finally, something he could sink his teeth into. He decided to revisit the Rutherford Ranch tomorrow and do two things. First, he would interview Paul Williamson who would be back from Cortez by then, and second, he would drive up to Burro Canyon and look around the area described by Jackson. He called the ranch, talked to Sarah Williamson and made an appointment for noon.

Rivera wanted to brief the sheriff on this new information, but couldn't. He was in Salt Lake City at a governor's conference for county sheriffs. So Rivera just went home.

He would forego breakfast at the diner tomorrow morning and eat a quick meal at home before going to the office. Then he'd make the long drive over the Castleton-Gateway road to the Rutherford Ranch. As he fed his guppies, he looked forward to tomorrow with anticipation, a feeling he hadn't had for some time.

12

RIVERA PULLED UP in front of the Rutherford ranch house just before noon and stepped out of his vehicle.

Paul Williamson stepped out on the porch. "Howdy, Deputy," he said with a grave expression. He was holding a mug of steaming coffee. "Come on in and have some coffee."

"Good morning, Mr. Williamson, and thanks, coffee sounds great."

The old man was in his usual place in the rocking chair. He rocked slowly and looked toward the horizon with the same watery stare he'd exhibited the first time Rivera had seen him. "Morning, Mr. Rutherford," Rivera said almost perfunctorily, as he followed Williamson into the ranch house. The screen door closed behind them with a clack.

They sat down at the kitchen table.

"Sarah told me you liked her sweet rolls, so she baked another batch this morning before she went to the children's home."

"Coffee and sweet rolls, my favorite meal," smiled Rivera. "I'll try not to take too much of your time, Mr. Williamson. I know how busy you must be around here."

"Please call me Paul. And yes, we're pretty busy these days. There's a new bull being hauled up here from Cortez later today, as well as a load of heifers. But take whatever time you need. Jesse was a good hand and we want his killer brought to justice. We miss him a great deal. Lots of work to do around here. We've already started looking for a replacement, just in case you hear of someone."

Rivera took a bite from a cinnamon bun and a sip of coffee. Then he got down to business. He questioned Williamson at length about Montoya's activities on the ranch, how he related to other people, what he did with his free time, and his use of drugs. Unfortunately, he was unable to learn anything he didn't already know.

"Did Montoya ever try to sell drugs to anyone here at the ranch?"

"Not to my knowledge. If I'd ever learned he was peddling dope, I'd have fired him on the spot. I was pretty sure he was a marijuana user, but it didn't affect his work. And as far as I know, he never lit up a joint while he was on the ranch. I guess smoking marijuana was something he did on his days off."

"He was a user all right. When we found his body, there were a couple of joints in his pocket. And traces of cocaine in his nostrils. What happened the day you left the ranch house in search of Montoya?"

"I saw a riderless horse coming in toward the ranch house. Eddie Stokes recognized it as Jesse's mount. We'd sent him out to Cottonwood Canyon earlier in the day to search for some cows and calves that had strayed from the herd and wandered up the canyon. I drove the truck up there to look for him, figuring his horse might've spooked and thrown him. Jesse was a decent horseman so I really wasn't sure what to think. But if he had gotten thrown, he might have needed medical help. I spent about five hours looking for him in the main canyon and its tributaries. There was no sign of him. It was getting dark and some thunderheads were moving in, so I finally came back to the ranch house. The next morning, I sent Eddie back up the canyon to look around some more. I had a commitment to meet some people at noon in Cortez on a cattle matter, so I left and drove down there. I called back to the ranch later that afternoon and got the bad news. What a damn shame. In the prime of his life."

"How far up the canyon did you go?" asked Rivera. Williamson seemed surprised by the question. "Why, all the way up to the end of the ranch. I turned around at the cattle guard and came back."

While Rivera was taking notes, he had a vague sense that Williamson was ill-at-ease. Maybe it was the lack of eye-contact or the cadence of his speech. Nervousness during an interrogation at the Sheriff's Department wasn't unusual, but the man was sitting in his own kitchen. However, Rivera considered, it's not every day a man's employee gets killed. That would be enough to stress out any employer. He decided Williamson's subtle signs of discomfort were probably not significant. He asked the ranch foreman a few more questions and, learning nothing new, told him that he was going back into the canyon to have another look around. He said goodbye, thanked him for the coffee and pastry, and headed down the porch steps to his pickup.

Rivera took the ranch road leading west into Cottonwood Canyon, continuing until he reached the mouth of Burro Canyon. There he turned left, drove in a short distance and stopped. He stepped out of his vehicle, closed the door, and looked into Burro Canyon. The canyon was flat and sandy to a width of about two hundred feet. It was populated by the usual plant community: juniper, sage, rabbitbrush and assorted grasses. A narrow cut down the middle of the canyon floor funneled the water produced by most rainfalls. The occasional heavy and extended thunderstorm would produce a torrent of water that would fill the canyon over its entire width. On each side of the canyon was a talus slope of fallen rock that slanted upward about a hundred feet to meet the red rock canyon walls which rose another five hundred feet straight up. Rivera spotted the large rock Randy

Jackson had mentioned and walked toward it, scanning the canyon in a cursory way, getting a feel for it. He decided the best approach would be to perform a grid search of the canyon floor over its entire width for a distance of fifty yards up-canyon and down-canyon from the large boulder. His plan was to walk in a straight line paralleling the canyon walls, scanning about three feet on either side of his path. After he'd completed a one-hundred yard segment this way, he would turn around, offset his path by six feet, and walk back to the other end. He would continue this pattern until he covered the entire area.

On the fifth pass he saw it. A small white potsherd with black markings. He picked it up by its edges and examined it. It appeared quite similar to the one extracted from Montoya's chest. Similar, he thought, but did it come from the same pot? He would lay them side by side and compare them when he got back to the office. He placed the fragment in a plastic evidence bag and marked the spot with a numbered yellow flag. He searched the immediate area for other sherds but found none. Then a glint of reflected light from the ground not far away caught his eye. It was a shell casing. He inserted his ballpoint pen into the open end and picked it up. The casing was from a nine-millimeter round, the same caliber as the bullet that had killed Montoya. He bagged it and marked the location with a second flag.

Rivera methodically continued his grid search for another hour, but found nothing else of interest. He returned to his truck and departed, certain he had uncovered material evidence. He drove up Cottonwood Canyon, across Fisher Valley, down the Onion Creek Road and back toward the office. As he drove he considered the possibility of asking the Utah State Police Forensics Lab in Price to come down and sweep the mouth of Burro Canyon for blood samples, but the rains which fell the evening after the murder had been so heavy that it would probably be a waste of everyone's time. He discarded the idea and focused on what he'd learned so far. It now seemed plausible Montoya had actually been killed in Burro Canyon and his body moved all the way up to the top of Cottonwood Canyon, some three miles away. And Jackson must have seen the killer carrying Montoya to the pickup truck. Facts were beginning to fit together and form a picture in Rivera's mind. The killer must have put Montoya's body in the passenger side of the truck, gone back to collect his hat, and driven from Burro Canyon up to the head of Cottonwood Canyon. It would therefore be likely that traces of Montoya's blood could be found in the killer's truck. The body and the hat were then dumped at the top of the canyon near its intersection with the Kokopelli trail, the place where the three bikers had found it.

But why kill a man and then move the body? He considered that but couldn't think of a good reason. Perhaps Burro Canyon was a regular exchange point for drug runners, and they wanted to protect it for future use. But that didn't make a lot of sense. It would be a simple matter to move the exchange point to another location. There were an unlimited number of remote places in and around the LaSal Mountains where a transaction could take place. Moving the body involved a much higher degree of risk than establishing a new exchange point. Very puzzling. Maybe the killing had nothing to do with the drug trade. But if it wasn't that, then what was it? Nothing came to mind. He decided he would have the shell casing and potsherd dusted for fingerprints. He would also compare the two pot fragments to see if, in fact, they had come from the same pot.

That evening, he sat in his office, considering his next step. He'd learned a few moments earlier that neither the shell casing nor the sherd had yielded any prints. He held up the two fragments and inspected them. They appeared to be the same color and the same material. If he could establish that the two pieces came from the same pot, then he would know with some certainty that Montoya had been killed in Burro Canyon and the body moved. His theory would advance from plausible to probable. He knew he couldn't personally make that determination. Tomorrow he would seek the advice of an expert.

Later, he briefed the sheriff on his activities over the past two days and what he'd learned.

"A few more steps, hopefully in the right direction," Bradshaw had said.

13

SORENSON WOKE UP in his motel room early in the morning and swung his legs over the side of the bed. He sat there for a moment, rubbing his eyes. Vague recollections of another bad dream lingered at the edge of his consciousness, but he couldn't remember anything specific. The muscles in his legs and back were stiff, no doubt a result of yesterday's long hike. He was accustomed to getting three or four days' rest between each trip to the cave, but now he was committed to doing three hikes on three successive days. And he'd done only the first day's hike. He let out a grunt as he stood up. After a long hot shower, his muscles began to feel more pliable. He dried himself off, got dressed, and performed a regimen of stretches.

He walked over to the window of his motel room, pushed aside the curtain, and peered outside. Another clear day. Good. He made his way to the small refrigerator in his room, removed a carton of orange juice, a bag of frozen blueberries, and a box of frozen sausage patties. He poured oatmeal into a plastic bowl, added water and a handful of blueberries, and heated it in the microwave oven. When that was ready, he placed three sausage patties into the microwave and cooked them on "high" for one minute. Breakfast was now ready. He consumed it quickly and checked his watch. Right on schedule.

He topped off his gas tank at the Texaco station on Main Street, paying in cash. Next came the long drive out to the Thompson Canyon Trail where he would park and start the journey down Cottonwood Canyon. As he drove upriver on Highway 128, he noticed in his rear-view mirror a sheriff's vehicle following along behind him. He set the cruise control on the speed limit. When he reached Castle Valley and made a right turn, the Sheriff's vehicle continued straight ahead on the main highway. Sorenson relaxed. The rest of the drive to the Thompson Canyon Trail was uneventful, but he found himself frequently glancing in the rear-view mirror. After he parked his vehicle in the usual place, he secured his handgun in the holster under his shirt, strapped on his backpack and began the long hike.

When he arrived at Burro Canyon, he put his new procedure into effect, carrying his backpack up the talus slope and into the cave. He ignited the propane lantern he'd left there and carefully retrieved the three pots Twitchell expected to receive at their rendezvous point later in the day. They were items #7, #36, and

#44 on the master list. He removed several sheets of bubble wrap and a roll of masking tape from his backpack. He picked up a 12-inch grey Anasazi pot with a corrugated finish, gently wrapped it, and taped it. He repeated the procedure with the second pot, a 10-inch black-on-white Mogollon bowl with the image of a coatimundi on the bottom and a series of parallel sawtooth lines around the lip. The third piece was an 8-inch buff-colored Hohokam pot. With each securely wrapped, he placed them into the three separate compartments of his backpack. He turned off the lantern and eased the backpack through the entryway to the cave, holding it out in front of him with care. Outside, after scanning the canyon, he strapped on the pack and descended the talus.

He was pleased the new procedure had worked so well. He marched out of Burro Canyon, turned left, and began the long trek up Cottonwood Canyon. But something was bothering him, something nebulous and unsettling in the back of his mind. He couldn't quite put his finger on it. It nagged at him while he hiked and he wondered why, with everything going according to plan, he felt an uneasiness.

A half-mile later it came to him. He realized he wasn't happy anymore. Before he'd found the cave, his life had been much simpler, much less stressful, and a lot more interesting. He'd been content. He used to sleep like a baby. He tried to console himself with the idea that this phase of his life would soon be over. He just needed to tough it out until the cave was emptied and its contents converted into cash. After that, he'd be able to start his life over. Maybe he'd leave Utah and move to a warmer climate. Change his identity. He could join one of those fancy country clubs and learn to play golf. Maybe even buy a home that backed up to a fairway. He forced himself to focus on a vision of life in which the days would be full of relaxation, contentment, and financial security. But as much as he tried, he couldn't completely escape the cloud of anxiety that hung over him.

He returned to his truck and began the drive out of the mountains and south to Cedar Mesa. There, the exchange with Twitchell took place without a hitch, his cash for the day totaling $28,400. He locked the bag of money in the truck's tool box alongside yesterday's proceeds.

Driving back to Moab, he listened to the radio. The local newscast mentioned the continuing search for Montoya's killer, but it had only gotten second billing to a story about an aggressive group of environmentalists trying to stop a new mining operation south of Moab. Maybe the hysteria about the killing was fading and with it the intensity of the sheriff's efforts. He believed the investigators had nothing substantial to go on, but he couldn't be sure. He would continue to empty the cave, carefully and steadily, without taking any foolish chances or yielding to impatience.

He had sold only about one third of the items in the cave and still had a long way to go.

14

MANNY RIVERA WAS so preoccupied with the Montoya case that he barely noticed the majestic Book Cliffs on the eastern horizon as he drove north on U.S. Route 6. For him, solving the case was like trying to assemble a jigsaw puzzle without having all the pieces. He had a few pieces, and maybe some of them fit together, but as yet he was unable to see the big picture. He was searching for a flow, an organizing principle, a sensible chronology that would tie everything together. Knowing for sure that the two sherds came from the same pot would be a big step in that direction. So he'd made an appointment for 1:00 P.M. to visit with Professor Edmund Hollingsworth at the University of Utah in Salt Lake City. It was fortuitous the professor was located so close by—he was a world-renowned scholar in anthropology with a specialty in American Indian pottery. Hopefully, the professor would shed some light on the two potsherds Rivera was bringing with him.

Earlier that morning at the Rim Rock Diner, Rivera had told Emmett Mitchell about the new find, and the problem posed by the two sherds. He'd explained that one had been found embedded in the victim's skin, the other near a 9-millimeter shell casing in Burro Canyon three miles from where the body had been found.

"I need to find out whether the two sherds came from the same pot. If they did, I'd be pretty sure Montoya was killed in Burro Canyon and his body moved. I also need to determine the origin of the pot and where geographically such artifacts are normally found."

"I know a professor at the University of Utah who would probably be able to answer those questions," said Mitchell. "His name is Edmund Hollingsworth. He taught my brother Frank several anthropology courses fifteen years ago. Frank was quite impressed by Hollingsworth, not only because of his extensive knowledge of anthropology, but also because of his excellent teaching skills. I met with him a few years later when I needed advice in connection with a museum theft. He was accommodating and provided many useful insights. Helped break the case."

"I'd like to talk to him," said Rivera.

Ten minutes later, Mitchell had called Hollingsworth and made arrangements for Rivera to visit him.

While on the subject of pottery during breakfast, Mitchell had also mentioned that the San Juan County

Sheriff's Office had received an FBI advisory requesting all law enforcement personnel be on the lookout for sources of illegally obtained Indian pottery. The Feds had learned from reputable collectors about a sudden increase in the merchandising of ceramic pots of questionable origin. The investigation was a high priority.

Mitchell went on. "As I'm sure you know, the FBI has jurisdiction whenever there's a violation of the Antiquities Act. Many ancient Indian graves on BLM land and the Indian reservations have been looted by pothunters over the years—unscrupulous individuals looking for pots, figurines, sandals, and anything of value that they can sell to collectors. The demand is high and so are the prices. The FBI is finally cracking down on violators, mainly in response to pressures from the Indian Nations. I think they're looking to set an example with a few convictions and some stiff sentences. It's probably not related to what you're working on, but I thought I'd mention it."

"Yeah, Sheriff Bradshaw received that same advisory. And Adam Dunne said each BLM office had gotten one."

As he drove through Price, Rivera sipped on the coffee he'd bought at McDonald's in Moab. The drive to Salt Lake City and back would take all day. He hoped he wasn't wasting precious time. After all, what did potsherds have to do with drug running?

He drove at the speed limit across the Wasatch Range. The cold nights of autumn had transformed the trees at the higher altitudes into a brilliant array of red, orange, and gold. It reminded him of a time when he was a boy. His father had taken him and his brothers and cousins to the Sacramento Mountains east of Las Cruces on their first camping trip. They'd explored and fished and camped out for four days. They learned how to gut fish and pan-fry them. As they sat around the campfire eating supper, his father would tell them stories of the old west, just as his father had told him. Some of his fondest memories were of those times spent with his father in the mountains.

He arrived at the University around noon and maneuvered his vehicle into a parking spot about a quarter-mile from the building that housed the Anthropology Department. Finding a parking space had not been easy. The map Mitchell had drawn for him showed a parking lot adjacent to the building, but that lot had been full. Every student seemed to have a car and any available parking space was like prey to a circling horde of predator vehicles. He walked toward his destination, glancing up at the mountains which towered over the city. What a beautiful site the Mormons had long ago chosen for their settlement.

Rivera opened the door to the Anthropology Department and entered. A woman looked up from her typing and smiled. She looked to be in her fifties, had shoulder-length dark hair, and wore glasses attached to a silver chain that hung around her neck.

"Good afternoon, Sir. May I help you?"

"Good afternoon. I'm Deputy Sheriff Manny Rivera. I have an appointment to see Dr. Hollingsworth."

"Oh, yes, he's expecting you. He's got someone in the office just now but he should be free in a minute. Would you like to take a seat on the couch until he's free?"

"Sure, thank you."

"I can offer you some decaf coffee," she said.

"Coffee sounds great. Thanks very much."

Rivera sipped his coffee and surveyed the waiting area. Framed photographs of ancient Indian dwellings and archaeological excavations hung on the walls as did shadow boxes containing potsherds and arrowheads. A locked cabinet with glass doors displayed a collection of ancient Indian pots and an assortment of spear points, bows, and atlatls. He'd come to the right place. He picked up an old copy of *The Anthropology and Education Quarterly* from the end table and thumbed through it as he waited. He could hear muffled voices coming from behind the professor's office door. Finally, the door opened and a young student with a sheen of perspiration on his face scurried out. The professor appeared next, spotted the deputy, and approached him.

"Good afternoon, Deputy Rivera. I'm Ed Hollingsworth." He greeted him with a smile and a strong handshake. Rivera judged the professor to be in his early sixties. He was blessed with a rugged handsomeness and an abundant crop of wavy white hair. He was about Rivera's size and had the weathered tan of a man who spent a lot of time outdoors. He wore a brown tweed jacket with leather pads on the elbows, and a white shirt with an open collar. Rivera took an instant liking to him.

"Let's go inside," Hollingsworth said. He led the deputy into the office and closed the door behind them. He sat down behind a large oak desk and motioned Rivera to sit in one of the rust-colored leather chairs in front of the desk. The shelves behind the professor were crammed full of books and magazines from the floor to the ceiling. Off to one side was a grey metal computer stand which supported a large-screen terminal currently displaying a graph of some kind. A printer sat quietly nearby. The desk had surprisingly little on it, just a calendar, a small stack of papers, a telephone, and an open book with yellow Post-It Notes protruding from several of its pages. There were two wooden trays, one marked "in," the other "out."

"Your desk is a whole lot neater than mine," observed Rivera, trying to get things started on a light note.

Hollingsworth smiled and leaned back in his chair, hands clasped behind his head. "It's by design. Years ago, my desk was always covered with piles of paper, files, and publications. Instead of just working on one thing, I'd have five or six partially completed tasks on my desk, each one distracting me from concentrating on any of the others. And I never could find what I needed in all those piles. Then a colleague of mine told me that a cluttered desk was the sign of a procrastinator. I thought about that for a while and decided he was right. Now I keep on my desk only the one thing I'm working on. I finish that and then move on to the next task. Things go faster that way."

"Good idea," said Rivera, picturing the mess of files and reports cluttering his own desktop.

"Of course, my administrative assistant keeps everything else I might need in her well-organized files out there," he said, motioning with his hand toward the reception area. "She feeds material to me as I need it. It's a good system."

There were a few more minutes of getting-acquainted talk about the university, the cost of an education, and the great lives that students lead, if only they realized it.

"I've always loved school," said Hollingsworth. "My college graduation was one of the saddest days of my life. I couldn't understand why my fellow students were cheering and celebrating so much on graduation day."

"What made you go into anthropology?" asked Rivera.

"My bachelor's degree was actually in ceramic engineering. After graduation, I went to California to work for an aerospace company in their advanced materials department. I was part of a group developing new ceramic components for aircraft propulsion systems. The assignments were interesting but I never really felt passionate about the work. Then one day I was visiting the Anasazi Heritage Center near Cortez, Colorado, and saw some ceramic pots made by the ancient Indians centuries ago. There was something about the pottery that resonated within me. I think it was the artistic aspect of the work—each piece reflected the individual taste of its maker. And each was unlike any other. This was an element which had always been lacking in my engineering work. Anyway, I became instantly hooked on the world of Indian artifacts and the people who created them. After that, I returned to school to earn a PhD in anthropology. I've been devoting my life to the study and interpretation of Indian artifacts ever since. It's a good life for me. I love hiking into remote areas, locating and excavating promising sites, and occasionally finding something that adds new perspective to what we know about how the Ancient Ones lived. And I love teaching."

The conversation then turned to Rivera, where he was from, and why he'd gotten into police work. They talked about Moab and the natural beauty of the canyon country that had induced Rivera to relocate to the area. Eventually they got around to the murdered man found there five days ago.

"Emmett Mitchell told me you'd be bringing some potsherds you'd like me to take a look at," said Hollingsworth. "It was good hearing from him. He's a first-class individual. And his brother was one of my top students."

Rivera extracted two clear plastic bags from a protective metal container in his shirt pocket. Each bag contained a sherd. He reached across the desk and handed them to the professor. Hollingsworth held the bags up, inspected them, and asked if he could remove the sherds from the bags. Rivera nodded and said they'd already been dusted for prints.

"Where did you find these?" asked the professor, selecting a magnifying glass from his desk drawer. Rivera told him.

"Hmm. They look like pieces from a Mimbres pot. I'd say they're nine hundred to a thousand years old. The pot was made using the coil method. Sherds from this type of pot are not commonly found in the area where you discovered them. The pot must have been recently broken, because the edges haven't been exposed to the elements for very long." His calloused fingers held one of the sherds out toward Rivera so he could inspect it. "You can see the difference in the shade of white along the edges as compared to the inside and outside faces."

Rivera hadn't noticed that. The professor held the two pieces next to each other, trying to see if any of the edges fit together. They didn't.

"They may or may not have come from the same pot. We'll go to the laboratory and ask our ceramics technician to run some tests. If the chemical constituents of the clay are identical, then they were made from clay taken from the same area. Considering where you found them, and the fact that sherds of this type are normally found in southern New Mexico, the probabilities would all but guarantee that they came from the same pot. If the two fragments are in fact from the same pot, and yet are not contiguous pieces, then, given that they were recently broken off, there should be some more sherds where these were found. Or at least, where the pot was broken."

Rivera was impressed with how much the professor was able to infer from such a brief inspection.

"Let's go to the lab," said Hollingsworth. The two men left the office and walked down a long hallway. "This ceramics lab is my pride and joy," Hollingsworth confided. "It was funded three years ago by a grant from the National Science Foundation. Now it's supported by annual contributions from a consortium of high-tech ceramics manufacturers interested in the history of ceramics." They passed several classrooms, a block of offices, and finally a section of small laboratories. The last door had "Ceramics Lab" stenciled across it.

"This place is pretty dusty. I hope you're not allergic. I can offer you a face mask if you'd like."

Rivera declined. The professor opened the door revealing a long narrow room with wooden lab benches running lengthwise on each side. The benches contained electronic instruments, cutters, centrifuges, washers, and other equipment. There was a myriad of potsherds, some partially assembled into pots, and many in numbered plastic bags. Ceramic dust lay everywhere. Several computer terminals, their keyboards caked with bits of clay, were interspersed among the instruments. Below the bench tops were wide flat drawers, an open one revealing more potsherds resting in small compartments, each compartment marked with an identifying code number. Above the benches were cabinets containing tools, scales, books, magazines, and notebooks. Two young men were working in the lab. The closer one, a bearded man in his late 20s who was wearing a black vinyl lab apron, was positioning a potsherd into some type of grinding device. The other occupant, a younger man, was working at a bench in the back of the lab. The bearded man, who seemed to be in charge, looked up, saw the professor, and came forward.

"Yes, Professor, can I help you?" He was chubby, unusually pale, and tended to avoid eye contact.

"Hi, William. This is Deputy Sheriff Rivera from Grand County. Down in the Moab area. He has a couple of potsherds with him. I'd like to get a mass spectrometer analysis on each of them. What we're after is a comparison that shows whether or not they were made from the same clay."

"Hello Deputy," said William, shyly offering his hand, then, seeing that it was covered with dust, quickly withdrawing it. "Sorry, Sir," he mumbled, blushing slightly.

Hollingsworth excused himself and left Rivera in William's hands. Explaining he had a seminar to teach for the next two hours, the professor indicated the lab work would take about an hour and a half. He would meet with the deputy back in his office after class to review and interpret the test results.

William got right to work, inspecting the sherds, cleaning them in an ultrasonic bath, and then inserting the first one into the mass spectrometer.

Rivera surveyed the lab, wondering what it would be like to spend a career working in a place like this. The rear windows admitted light, but not much of the outside world could be seen. The glass was caked with a grey dust. He was thankful his job allowed him to spend time outdoors in the fresh air. He suddenly realized he was holding his breath, trying to stifle a sneeze. He extracted his handkerchief and blew his nose. Breathing once again, he continued looking around the lab as he waited. He noticed the young man in the back of the lab inspecting and selecting sherds from an array that he had laid out on the bench top. He had cemented most of them together into an almost-complete terra-cotta pot. Rivera was interested and wanted to watch his technique, but he started sneezing and for a time was unable to stop. When he got control of himself, he asked William how long the measurements would take.

"I should be through about three thirty, Sir," William said, keeping his eyes on his work.

"I'll come back then. This dust is getting to me." Rivera left the lab and exited the building, in search of fresh air.

Outside, he killed time by walking around the campus. It was a beautiful place, with contemporary buildings and well-maintained lawns, set on the east bench of the Salt Lake Valley against the backdrop of the Wasatch Mountains. In the plaza of the Student Union, he sat down and relaxed on a wooden bench that faced the mountains. Some students were throwing Frisbees on the expanse of lawn in front of him, some were sunbathing. A group of four coeds approached. They passed by, looked him over, whispered, and giggled as they departed. Rivera smiled. The whole scene reminded him of when he was a student at New Mexico State University in Las Cruces. The professor was right. Most college kids didn't realize how lucky they were to be leading the life of a student. There's academic pressure of course, but it's also four years of fun, friendships, and learning new things. Rivera had been the first one in his family to graduate from college. He'd chosen criminal justice as his career field, having always had the desire to make a contribution to his community and earn the respect of his neighbors. He recalled how proud his mother and father had been on his graduation day. They'd organized a backyard celebration in his honor with barbecued beef, tamales, beer, and desserts arranged on long tables with white tablecloths. All of his relatives, friends, and neighbors were in attendance. It was a day he would never forget.

15

RIVERA GLANCED AT his watch, got up from the bench, and spent a little more time wandering around the campus. When it was time to return, he walked back to the Anthropology Department, eager to see the results of the tests. He entered the Ceramics Lab and stifled a sneeze as he greeted William.

"How are the tests going?"

"I'm just about done," said William. The two sherds were back in their plastic bags and a printer was chattering. "We'll have the results in a minute or two. We need a new printer. This old one is a real clunker. Way too slow."

Rivera was glad this was almost over. He enjoyed learning about the laboratory and its operations but didn't enjoy breathing its air. As he waited for the printout, he wandered toward the rear of the lab where the younger man, whose name was Dennis, was completing the reassembly of the terra-cotta pot. He looked at the man's work, admiring its precision.

"Where's that pot from?" asked Rivera.

"Oh, it was made here in the lab as part of a special project. Grad students make pots, then break and reassemble them for practice. It helps them understand not only how pots were made, but also in what patterns they break into pieces. And it allows them to practice reassembly without risking actual ancient sherds. I'm doing this work to provide some good examples of proper reassembly. Reassembly is my specialty." He pointed to a shelf above his work bench. "I did those two pots up there. The black one with the three white stripes was made, broken and reassembled here. The white one with the black markings is a genuine ancient pot."

Rivera looked at the other two pots that Dennis had reassembled. The white pot with the black markings caught his attention immediately. There were two pieces missing from an otherwise complete pot. Rivera froze, staring in disbelief. He was speechless. Could it be?

At that moment William arrived at the back of the lab. "It looks like your two sherds were made from the same clay." He handed the two bagged sherds and a computer printout to Rivera. "The professor can give you a more detailed interpretation of . . ." He stopped in mid-sentence when he saw the expression on Rivera's face.

The deputy removed the two sherds from their bags and held them up to the reconstructed pot, confirming that they indeed matched the shapes of the missing pieces. The black markings lined up perfectly.

"I'll be damned!" said Rivera. He turned to Dennis. "Where did you get the pieces to make this pot?"

"Frank Sorenson, one of our graduate students in anthropology, brought me the sherds last Tuesday. He said an associate of his from another university uncovered the pot at an archaeological dig. An undergraduate who was wrapping it for transport accidentally dropped it and it shattered. Frank asked me to reconstruct the pot. Said he'd pay me two hundred dollars. I told him I can always use some extra money. Did I do something wrong?"

"No, no. You've done nothing wrong. But I need to talk to this Frank Sorenson. Do you know where I can find him?"

"I haven't seen him since the day he brought me the sherds. That was about a week ago," said Dennis.

I haven't seen him since that day either," added William. "Professor Hollingsworth is his advisor. Maybe he can help you locate him."

Rivera looked at his watch, thought for a moment. "I need to take this pot with me. It may be evidence in a murder case." Both young men listened with eyes wide open and faces frozen. Rivera continued, "Has the cement holding the pot together hardened enough for me to handle it?"

Dennis responded. "I reassembled it yesterday so the cement will be plenty hard by now. The pot is stronger now than before it was broken. But the individual sherds are fragile. I recommend we wrap it in something soft for you and that you handle it gently."

William and Dennis, with puzzled expressions but apparently not wanting to ask the deputy a lot of questions, worked in silence. They wrapped the pot in a cotton cloth and then added two layers of plastic bubble-wrap. They placed it in a small cardboard box and added pieces of foam rubber to keep it stationary within the box.

Rivera thanked the two technicians for their invaluable help. He left the laboratory, walked down the hall to the professor's office, and waited for him to return.

As soon as Hollingsworth walked into the office, Rivera stood up and began filling him in on what had taken place. The box was resting on Hollingsworth's desk. The professor peeled back the bubble wrap and inspected the pot. He raised his eyebrows. Rivera continued. "I need to get in touch with Frank Sorenson right away to find out when and where he found the sherds."

"I haven't seen Frank in a week or so," said the professor, holding the two fragments up to the pot. "I have no idea where he is." He sat down in his chair, appearing pensive. "I think at this point it would be wise to call in the University Provost." Hollingsworth made the call and told the provost that he had a rather urgent situation involving the police and asked if he could come over right away.

While the two men waited for the provost to arrive, Hollingsworth told Rivera everything he knew about Sorenson. "He's an older student, in his fifties. He got his bachelor's degree in anthropology here a couple of years ago and is now pursuing his master's degree. He's finished all the necessary coursework and is working on his thesis. His interest is Basketmaker pottery from the San Rafael Swell. He's a very good student. Grade point average is around 3.7."

Rivera was jotting the information into his notepad. One step at a time, he thought.

Hollingsworth continued, "Sorenson's a likeable fellow. He's quiet, works hard, and is serious about his studies. Seems to have finally found what he wants to do with his life. A little later than most, but he's found it nonetheless. Since he's completed all his coursework, he doesn't come around here much anymore. He's often out on a dig or doing research in the library. I do recall he was in here several weeks ago, asking questions about our PhD program. He said he's thinking about teaching anthropology. He also has a job working part-time as a student assistant for Professor Harold Jenkins in the History Department. Maybe Jenkins can add to what I've told you."

About that time the provost entered the office. He was a tall man in a grey suit with a full head of dark hair, side-parted and shiny. He had an officious bearing and a commanding presence. After introductions, the provost was briefed on the situation. He made a phone call and ten minutes later, a young clerk, pretty and blond, hurried into the office with a file. She handed it to the provost, glancing furtively at Rivera as she departed.

The provost studied the contents of the file. "He has an office over in the History Department where he works for Professor Jenkins. I'll call there now to see if he's in." He dialed the number, waited a moment, and hung up. "He's not in his office. I'll try Professor Jenkins. Maybe he knows where he is." After a brief conversation the provost returned the telephone to its cradle. "Jenkins wasn't in his office either but the department's administrative assistant said Sorenson hasn't been in his office for several days. She said his job is to collect and sort sources of historical information for Jenkins. According to the A.A., Jenkins has been looking for him. He has a backlog of research material for Sorenson to review and hasn't been too happy about his assistant's absence."

The provost thought for a moment. "Perhaps he's at home." He consulted the file again. "He lives in Vista Village, a small community of older duplexes about three blocks from the university. The units are rented mostly by students. You can call him or drive over there." He read off Sorenson's home address and phone number which Rivera recorded in his notepad.

"I'll drive over," said the deputy. "And I'll need to take that pot with me as evidence."

The provost said that would be no problem but he would need a hand receipt for the University's records. He extracted a photograph of Sorenson from the file and gave it to Rivera. "This is what he looks like. You can keep the photo—there are several more like it in the file. According to his records, he's a good student. He's completed all his coursework for a master's degree in anthropology and lacks only his thesis." He closed the file. "I'm sorry, I have to get back to my office now to meet with some visitors from Washington. I'll give you one of my business cards." He wrote his home phone number on the back and gave it to Rivera. "Call me any time, day or night, if I can be of further assistance."

Rivera wrote out a hand receipt for the pot, added one of his own cards, and gave them to the provost. "Thanks for your help," he said. "And I'd appreciate it if the university staff would keep all this confidential for now." They shook hands and the provost departed.

Before Rivera left Hollingsworth's office, the professor sketched out a map showing the best way to get to Vista Village. The deputy thanked him for his expert assistance and hospitality. Hollingsworth smiled warmly and shook Rivera's hand. He said he was happy to oblige and hoped their paths would cross again.

Rivera returned to his vehicle. He got in and sat there, thinking. He'd found two more pieces to the puzzle. First, the two sherds were from the same pot, so Montoya was definitely killed in Burro Canyon. And second, Sorenson had been given the sherds that completed the original pot by a fellow archaeologist from another university. These two facts posed a series of questions. Why had Montoya's body been moved? If Burro Canyon was an exchange point for illegal drugs, what was so special about it? Instead of moving the body, why not just change the location? That part made little sense. Maybe the drug premise was wrong. But if the crime wasn't about drugs, then what was it about? The lower part of Burro Canyon was on the Rutherford Ranch. Was it possible that Montoya was moved just to get him off ranch property? Could Mr. Rutherford have had him killed for some reason? Or the foreman, Mr. Williamson? That didn't seem likely. Mr. Rutherford was approaching senility and Mr. and Mrs. Williamson were model citizens of the community. And all ranch personnel had clean records.

His thinking moved back to the sherds. Sorenson had told Dennis that the shattered pot had come from an archaeological dig. According to Hollingsworth, Mimbres pots were found only in southern New Mexico. So if the pot was broken there, and the sherds given to Sorenson, how did the two missing pieces end up in the canyons of Grand County, Utah?

Rivera turned the ignition key and started the engine. Sorenson might be able to answer that last question. So finding him was now priority one. Following the hand-drawn map, Rivera drove toward Vista Village. More questions tumbled around in his mind. Was there a reason for Sorenson's archaeological associate to lie about the source of the sherds? Perhaps he had stolen the pot, then had accidentally broken it. Or perhaps Sorenson himself had lied about the sherds. But that didn't seem consistent with Hollingsworth's description of the man.

Rivera pulled up in front of Sorenson's residence. It was one-half of a small white clapboard duplex, probably built in the 1940s. There were dozens of them in the neighborhood, all identical. He found Unit 16A and knocked on the door. Waited. Knocked again. No answer. He stepped over to the other side of the duplex and knocked on the door marked 16B. A young brunette co-ed in cut-off jeans and a tank top opened the door. Rivera introduced himself and asked if she knew the man who lived next door.

"Frank? Sure. We call him Grandpa." She emitted a delightful high-pitched staccato laugh. "He's a great guy. Always giving us younger students advice on how to lead good lives. Productive lives. He's probably the oldest student in the school. Always working or studying. Never parties. Is he in trouble?"

"No, no, not at all. We think he may have some information that would help us in an investigation. He's not at home. Have you seen him today?"

"No, actually we haven't seen him for several days. Robert, he's my roommate, was wondering just this morning where Frank was. His pickup truck's been gone. He always parks it right out front when he's here. He's an anthropology student, so we figured he was out playing in the dirt at one of his digs." She laughed again.

"What color is his pickup truck?" Rivera was thinking about the tan or grey pickup that Jackson had seen in Burro Canyon.

"Bright red," she replied.

Rivera left his business card and asked her to call him confidentially on his cell phone if she learned anything about Sorenson's whereabouts. He returned to his vehicle, called the BLM Field Office in Moab, and asked to speak with Adam Dunne. Dunne wasn't in the office, but Rivera was able to reach him in Monticello via his cell phone.

"Still chasing unruly environmentalists?"

Dunne laughed. "Nah. I think we've got all that under control. They're a bunch of good kids who just wanted to demonstrate in front of the mine. Placards and chants and all that. But a couple of older trouble-makers tried to co-opt a legitimate movement for their own purposes. They were being paid by a local land-owner who didn't want to see the mine reopened. It's all finished. The bad guys lost."

"I need to find out about archaeological digs on BLM land—how all that works. How you get a permit. Who keeps the records. So forth."

"I can help you out, but once again, you'll owe me big. I'll just add this to the long list of favors you'll never repay."

Rivera laughed. "Hey, don't forget. That corpse was found on BLM land—your domain. I'm actually doing your work for you."

"Okay, here's the way it works. Two documents are required before an archaeological dig can proceed on BLM land. First, a general permit is required to ensure the applicant has the experience and education appropriate to the work. This is called a Cultural Use Resource Permit. Normally organizations such as universities apply for these to establish that they have the basic qualifications needed to execute a proper dig and document the results. The application is made by the organization's permit administrator. Then, when a specific site is identified for a prospective dig, a Field Use Authorization is required. This document allows a BLM Field Office archaeologist to evaluate and assess the purpose, plan, and personnel for a specific dig. He has the authority to approve or deny the request. The records are maintained at the BLM Field Office in whose district the work would take place. For Cottonwood Canyon, for example, that would be the Moab office."

Rivera then recounted for Dunne the story of what he'd discovered at the Ceramics Laboratory, Hollingsworth's analysis of the sherds, and why it was important to find a student named Frank Sorenson.

"Interesting," said Dunne. "I'm sure the University of Utah has a general permit—most universities with archaeological departments do. But maybe I can find out for you if Sorenson's name appears on any of the Field Use Authorizations and where those sites are located. Let me do a little research and call you back."

"Thanks, Adam."

The sky to the west had become a rich shade of crimson and the temperature was dropping fast. Rivera decided to check into a motel and spend the night in Salt Lake City. Tomorrow he would continue his search for Sorenson.

Later that evening, Rivera sat in his room watching the evening news, hoping his cell phone would ring. At 8:23 P.M., the call came.

"Okay, Manny. First of all, the University of Utah does have a Cultural Resource Use Permit for BLM lands in Utah, Arizona, New Mexico, Colorado, and Wyoming. No surprise. And Frank Sorenson's name is listed on seven Field Use Authorizations. It turns out all seven are located in the San Rafael Swell area. I also checked with our Field Offices in southern New Mexico. They have no record of him down there. So if the pot came from the Mimbres zone, Sorenson wasn't part of the dig."

"The San Rafael Swell. That's the area of his thesis research. It's nowhere near Cottonwood Canyon."

"Right. And before you ask, no Field Use Authorizations have been requested or issued for Cottonwood Canyon or Burro Canyon in the last ten years."

16

THE SUN WAS descending behind the Abajo Mountains and the last shadows of the day were lengthening across Route 191 as Sorenson drove north toward Moab. He'd successfully completed the third and last day of his pot-selling marathon. Earlier in the day, he'd noticed the trek to the cave and back had been surprisingly easy. Maybe all the hiking was getting him back into shape. Not quite like his Army days, but he felt in better shape than he had in years. Today's exchange of pots for cash had added another $17,100 to his toolbox-turned-bank. Execution of the plan had once again been flawless and Twitchell seemed to be moving the merchandise without much difficulty.

He pulled into the Shell station in Monticello to fill his gas tank and buy an apple and a diet Dr. Pepper. He paid in cash, always careful to minimize his paper trail. As he walked back to the truck, he noticed again the increase in his leg strength and lung capacity. He wasn't tired in the least; in fact, he felt rather energized. He decided then that instead of returning to Salt Lake

City, he would stay in Moab tonight, call Twitchell, and attempt to set up two more runs. *As long as I'm feeling this strong and the merchandise is moving so well, why not just continue?* If Twitchell was willing and able, he would transfer three items to him tomorrow and three the next day.

That evening, Sorenson walked to a public telephone in Moab and dialed Twitchell's number. When the artifact trader answered, Sorenson told him he could make two more deliveries, one tomorrow and one the day after. Twitchell laughed.

"All this driving is wearing me out—but okay, I'll be there."

"Make it 2:00 P.M., both days," said Sorenson.

Twitchell selected three items from the master list for tomorrow and three for the following day. "I've got buyers waiting for these items so I can move them quickly."

Sorenson picked up some grilled chicken and a salad at the City Market in Moab. He rented a room for two more nights at the same motel, prepaying in cash. Lying in bed, eating and watching the weather man on TV, his thoughts turned to Twitchell. The trader had an air of understated competence. And he seemed to be a man of his word. Crooked and honorable at the same time. Even though he'd never met the man face-to-face, he was beginning to like him.

He finished his supper, turned off the TV and set the alarm for 6:00 A.M. Before he dozed off, he thought again about the day when this would be over, when all of the cave's contents had been removed and sold. Perhaps another month. Then he would be able to relax.

17

THE PROVOST INSERTED his master key into the lock of Frank Sorenson's office door, unlocked it, and pushed it open. He stepped aside and allowed Rivera to enter.

"Everything in here is university property, and you have my permission to examine all of it. If Sorenson can help in your investigation, then by all means we want to assist you in locating him." The provost selected another master key from his key ring and unlocked Sorenson's desk. He looked around the office and shook his head. "I hope you're able to find something useful in all this mess." He looked at his watch. "I have to get back to the office for a staff meeting. Call me anytime I can be of assistance."

Earlier that morning, Rivera had checked out of his motel and driven back to Sorenson's residence, finding it was still unoccupied. Disappointed, he knew his investigation was at a standstill until he could locate him and determine where he'd obtained the sherds for the reassembled pot. He'd briefly considered trying to obtain a search warrant for the house but decided that no judge in the state would issue one. Sorenson was not a suspect and was being sought only because he might have information useful in an investigation. But searching Sorenson's office was another matter—that was the university's domain. He'd called the provost who was happy to cooperate, and now Rivera found himself looking around at the meager trappings of a student assistant's office.

The tiny room contained a grey metal desk piled high with stacks of papers, technical journals, and re-ports. An old black telephone rested atop one of the piles. Behind the desk was a swivel chair with green cushions worn threadbare. A white plastic visitor's chair sat alongside the desk. Grey metal bookshelves full of books, magazines, and notebooks concealed two of the office walls. Two dozen cardboard boxes containing old books occupied most of the available floor space. There were no windows and the smell of mildew permeated the air. Rivera hoped that somewhere in this jumble he would find a clue to Sorenson's whereabouts. Or even better, that Sorenson would shortly walk through the door and introduce himself.

Rivera scanned the desktop. On top of a pile of *American Anthropologist* magazines was an appointment book containing one page for each month. He flipped through the pages until he reached the current month, October. The last entry was ten days ago and it simply stated *Out of Town*. He turned the page and scanned the November schedule. Here, several meetings with his thesis advisor had been scheduled. The last one bore the notation *Thesis Plan - Final OK?* which had been underlined twice. Rivera scanned the pages preceding October. On the first day of each month there was the notation *Pay Rent*. Several entries simply said *Out of Town*. Others denoted book auctions in various cities, primarily in Utah and Colorado. A few entries said *San Rafael Swell*. But Rivera found nothing particularly useful.

He continued searching. The desk had four drawers: a shallow center drawer and three deeper ones in the right pedestal. The center drawer contained the usual items: pens, pencils, paper clips, a tape dispenser, a magnifying glass, and a small stapler. It also contained numerous clear plastic bags containing potsherds. Each bag had an adhesive strip annotated with information related to general location, GPS coordinates, date, and type. The fragments had been uncovered at dozens of sites in Utah. However, none appeared similar to the Mimbres sherds of interest to Rivera.

He closed the center drawer and slid open the top drawer of the pedestal. Inside, he found typed and handwritten pages related to Sorenson's thesis. The working title was *"Comparative Interpretations of Basketmaker Pottery Designs Found in the Lower San Rafael Swell."* The area was west of Moab on the other side of the Green River. He remembered Emmett Mitchell saying he'd camped out there in his younger days. He'd said it was about 3000 square miles of eroded upthrust, an area of stark and rugged beauty. The drawer also contained several well-worn maps of the Swell and dozens of photographs showing various types of petroglyphs and pictographs. There was also a file containing copies of emails between Sorenson and his advisor, Dr. Hollingsworth.

He closed the top drawer and pulled open the second one. It contained items related to Sorenson's work for the history professor. There were brochures describing auctions of book collections, notices of estate sales, handwritten lists of book titles, copies of correspondence with Professor Jenkins, and several rare book catalogs. Nothing that hinted at Sorenson's whereabouts. He picked up the office phone and called Sorenson's residence on the chance he might have returned. As he listened to the phone ringing, he opened the third drawer and began inspecting its contents. The ringing continued with no answer. He hung up.

In the front of the third drawer, he found a bundle of maps secured by a rubber band. Included were Utah state maps, roadmaps of Uintah and Duchesne Counties, and USGS maps describing areas within Grand County and San Juan County. They were well-worn and gritty with the fine red sand common to those areas. He set them aside and removed a stack of receipts held together with a large paper clip. He flipped through them, noted nothing unusual, and placed them on top of the desk. Next was a pile of bank statements held together with a rubber band. He set these on the desktop next to the receipts. He picked up a file containing three loose handwritten sheets of paper, apparently torn from some kind of journal. Rivera was beginning to get the feeling that the office search was coming up empty. Just then, the office door swung open and a man appeared.

"I'm Professor Jenkins. Any sign of Sorenson yet?" he asked, omitting any form of greeting. He was a younger man, lean, and of average height. He wore a dark suit and a yellow bow tie. He had black hair and his chin jutted out in a challenging manner. His attitude suggested he considered himself superior to mere mortals. Rivera disliked him right off, but remained professional.

"No, nothing yet. He hasn't been at his residence for the past few days. The provost gave me permission to go through his office. I'm trying to get a lead on where he might be. It's important that I talk to him. And soon."

"Yes, I know all that," said Jenkins, dismissing the subject with a sweep of his hand. "The provost called and briefed me."

"The provost said Sorenson works for you as a student assistant. What can you tell me about his work assignment?"

"My field is history. In particular, I specialize in the history of the Four Corners area during the late nineteenth and early twentieth centuries. There's a lot of source material hidden away in people's trunks, attics, and basements that has the potential to shed more light on what was going on around here back then. The area's always been sparsely populated, but its development is interesting because of the crosscurrents of the many cultures that inhabited the area. Mormon settlers, Utes, Navajos, various Pueblo tribes, Hispanics, Canadian fur trappers, Anglo settlers pushing west. Each group affected the cultural development of the others in ways I find interesting. Then you have the emergence of commercial and industrial activities peculiar to the high desert. Dry farming or farming with irrigation water channeled from mountain snowmelt. Cattle ranching in the valleys during the winter. Cowhands driving the animals to the mesa tops and mountains for better grazing during the summer. Prospecting and mining the ore-producing strata for coal, copper, iron, bentonite, and so forth. Uranium, vanadium, and molybdenum came later."

Rivera noticed that the professor's demeanor was slowly changing from curt and condescending to enthusiastic and engaging as he spoke about the subject he loved.

"The fundamental question for me involves the cultural interactions and how they affected and enhanced the lives of individuals in each group. So I need details of the everyday activities and thoughts of individuals and families to put together an aggregate picture. I find out-of-print history books, newspaper articles, municipal files, business accounts, personal journals, and family records to be rich sources of information that help me in understanding how community life evolved out here. I use Sorenson to attend estate auctions and bookstore clearance sales for me. My NSF grants help pay his salary. He buys collections that might contain information helpful to my research. Then he scans and sorts the material, setting aside the useful documents for me to review and reselling the rest. He's become quite proficient at it but lately he's gone too much of the time. His attendance has been erratic for the last couple of months. Just look at this office. It's crammed with items he's acquired for me but he's way behind on reviewing and cataloguing them. I may have to replace him."

"When was the last time you saw him?" asked Rivera.

"About ten days ago. He was in here working for a while but left without a word to anyone."

"Yeah, his calendar just says *Out of Town*. Any idea where he might have gone?"

"Who knows? It's possible he's somewhere out in the San Rafael Swell doing research for his thesis. If you find him, tell him if he doesn't come back soon, he'll be fired." The professor, now having completely reverted back to his earlier disposition, turned on his heel and departed without another word.

Rivera sat there and slowly shook his head. He felt sorry for Sorenson. His appreciation of Sheriff Bradshaw as a boss clicked up another notch.

He returned to the task at hand and glanced at the sheets of paper in the file he was still holding. The pages were old and the ink was faded. Probably some historical reference material. As he started to close the file and return it to the desk drawer, his eyes caught the words *collection of old Indian pots* on the first sheet. He studied the papers. They appeared to be pages torn from an old diary. The top page was dated May 28th. The year was not given. He read the entry:

May 28th

Dear Diary,

A letter from Liam arrived today. It makes me so happy when I hear from him! I check the mailbox every day. He's on my mind every hour of every day. Just thinking about him makes me happy, but I'd be even happier if we were together.

Anyway he told me about a trip he and his best friend Josh Cummings took to a secret cave where Josh had stored his collection of old Indian pots and figurines. Liam seemed to relish giving me all the details of the route they took, and how very long and arduous it was. Some of it was on horseback and some of it on foot. It all sounded very exciting and very mysterious. He said it was a big secret. Of course I'll never tell anyone. It'll be our secret, dear diary.

I can't wait until we're married and spending each day together. Liam thinks we should wait until we have enough money saved to buy our own place. I know he's probably right, but maybe we could get by on less and enjoy being together now. But if Liam thinks we should wait, we'll wait. With what he earns as a ranch hand and my income from teaching, we should be able to marry in a year or two. It just seems like forever.

I'll write Liam a long letter on Saturday. Maybe I'll suggest that we shouldn't wait. I know he wants to do right by me, give me a proper home and all, but I just want to be with him!

Becky

He read the other pages. There were two more of them, each a separate diary entry written during the same month, and each similar in content.

He extracted the last item from the drawer, a manila folder containing two sheets of paper. Both were photocopies. The first had a column of numbers from one to thirty-two with a dollar figure next to each number. The dollar figures varied, but all were quite large, several thousand dollars each. The second sheet was similar, the numbers continuing from thirty-three to fifty-four. A red pencil had been used to draw a line through nineteen of the numbers.

Rivera now took a greater interest in the bundle of bank statements resting on the desk. He removed the rubber band and studied them. The accounts, in the name of Frank Sorenson, were with three Salt Lake City banks. All three were initiated about two months ago, and each showed large deposits since then. After some mental arithmetic, Rivera could see that the total of all the deposits roughly corresponded to the total of the amounts on the list which had been red-lined.

The chair squeaked as Rivera leaned back and stared at the ceiling. So, he thought, an older student assistant suddenly comes into a significant stream of cash at about the same time his work attendance becomes erratic. Add to that the reconstructed pot in the ceramics lab with two pieces missing, the very pieces found in the victim's chest and at the scene of the crime in Burro Canyon. Then add these pages torn from an old diary that talks about a cave containing a collection of Indian artifacts. Could Sorenson have somehow found that cave? And after all these years, were the pots and figurines still there? Of course, there was no hard evidence to show Montoya's killing was directly related to any of this. He could have simply fallen on a potsherd during a drug-related squabble that had ended in his death. And it was possible that everything Sorenson had done was perfectly legitimate.

If the cave actually existed and contained items of great value, then where was it? If it was on private land and if Sorenson had the permission of the owner to sell the artifacts, then he'd done nothing wrong. If the cave was on government land, then that was another matter entirely. So the next order of business would be to determine the exact location of the cave. Or, even better, find Sorenson and ask him.

Rivera again read the pages torn from the diary. He wondered who Becky was. Maybe the rest of the diary was somewhere in the office. He got up and began inspecting the boxes full of books. It didn't take him long to find the diary. In fact, there was a set of fifteen, each with a blue cloth cover faded with the passage of time. He'd found them in a box of books marked *Ready for Professor's Review*. The diaries were all the same type, each containing enough pages to allow daily entries for a full year. The first one in the series was dated 1925. The name written inside the front cover of each diary was Rebecca Ann Cross of Colorado Springs, Colorado. The diaries from 1925 to 1937 were completely filled with entries, but the 1938 diary was complete only through December 11th. The last diary, the one for 1939, was completely blank. Since the handwriting matured with the passing years, it was a simple matter for Rivera to find the diary from which the pages had been torn. It was the 1938 diary. He decided to scan that volume, particularly the days just before and just after the May

28th entry, looking for other references to the cave and hopefully its location.

He returned to the chair, sat down, and cleared a small corner of the desk. He leaned back, put his feet up and began reading. As he turned the pages, he found he couldn't put the diary down. He saw a picture of a young lady's life in great personal detail. The joy of a budding romance and a hoped-for marriage, the excitement of the little things in her everyday life, her happy home life and her love of teaching, and the letters from Liam she cherished so much. Her life ahead of her, full of wonderful possibilities and exciting expectations. And then the loss, the feeling of abandonment, the sadness, the withdrawal, and finally the emptiness. Becky's anguish pained him. He reread the last entry:

Dec. 11th

Dear Diary,

Mother is right. I must face facts. Liam is gone and he's not coming back. I feel so very sad and empty. Is he dead or did he just change his mind about me? I miss him so much. I don't know what I'll do with my life now.

Becky

Rivera put the diary down. No wonder Professor Jenkins was so interested in first-hand historical accounts. They contained so much real-life information—not just facts, but also how people reacted to events, how they felt about things. Here was a day-by-day story about a girl's life torn apart by the disappearance of her fiancé who vanished without a word. But there was no further mention of the cave. He wasn't surprised, having concluded by now that all of the pages referring to the Indian artifacts had been removed by Sorenson so Professor Jenkins's eyes would never behold them.

He reread the first page torn from the diary, focusing on the paragraph in which Becky described the letter she'd received from Liam. Evidently that particular letter had provided specific details of the route Liam and Josh had used to arrive at the secret cave. Sorenson, if he'd somehow found Liam's old letters, might have been able to locate the cave. The pots would be highly valuable by today's standards. And that would account for the large bank deposits.

Rivera began searching the office for the letters. But he didn't really expect to find them. If they had been there, they most likely would have been in the desk's bottom drawer. They certainly wouldn't be with the material scheduled for review by Professor Jenkins. Possibly they were in Sorenson's home. Or he might have destroyed them. Why keep them after you know the location of the cave? Rivera, despite his misgivings, made a thorough search. As expected, the letters were not in the office.

He wondered if he might be at a dead end. If only Sorenson would show up, his questions would be answered. But the man was nowhere to be found. So now, Rivera had to find the letters or find someone familiar with their contents. Becky had read the letters but she was probably no longer alive. And if she was, she'd be in her nineties and might have long ago forgotten what Liam had said in his letters. But everything had to be checked and maybe, if she *was* still alive, she would remember. And so, the next step was to determine what had become of Rebecca Ann Cross.

After an hour of telephoning from Sorenson's office, and with the help of research he'd enlisted from the Grand County Sheriff's Office and the FBI, Rivera learned that Rebecca Ann Cross was indeed still alive. She resided in an assisted-living facility called the Cenizo Home for the Elderly which was located in Vernal, Utah. He called the home, identified himself, and asked to speak to the director.

"This is Mr. Fielding. How may I be of service?"

"Hello Mr. Fielding. This is Deputy Sheriff Manuel Rivera of the Grand County Sheriff's Department. We're investigating a homicide, and I would like to speak with Rebecca Ann Cross, but first I wanted to get some background information about her."

"Oh dear. A *homicide?* And this might have something to do with *our Rebecca?*" asked the director in an incredulous tone.

Rivera assured him this was indeed the case, as astounding as it may seem. "Now what can you tell me about Rebecca," he reiterated.

The director cleared his throat. "Well, first of all deputy, Rebecca hasn't spoken a word in years. She's quite elderly, 94-years old, but she's alert and seems to have all of her faculties. She spends a lot of time alone in her room, looking out the window. Our staff psychologist says that her mind is locked onto something that happened long ago. She's basically living in the past. But she's healthy, eats all her meals, and always has a pleasant disposition. And she's very kind. I often see her helping other residents in thoughtful ways. She's fastidious about her appearance and her personal hygiene. She's really a model resident."

Rivera digested the information. "Does she have any relatives or regular visitors?"

"Oh yes. Rebecca never married and has no children, but her nephew and his wife look after her. They're a very nice couple, in their mid-sixties, I would say. They help pay her bills as best they can and visit with her every week."

"I'd like to talk to them. Can you tell me how to get in touch?"

"Of course. They live right here in Vernal. Their names are Kenneth and Jill Vance." Fielding gave Rivera the address and phone number.

Before leaving Sorenson's office, Rivera made three more phone calls. The first one was to the Vance residence to make an appointment to visit later in the day. The second was to the provost to brief him on what he'd learned and to tell him that he was removing certain items from Sorenson's office that might be relevant to the investigation. A receipt was being forwarded to him via the History Department's administrative assistant. The third call was to Sheriff Bradshaw to update him on the case.

Rivera left Sorenson's office, strode back to his vehicle, and departed Salt Lake City heading for Vernal. After he'd escaped the city traffic and was driving on U.S. 40 across the Wasatch Mountains, he reflected on his telephone conversation with the sheriff. He thought he'd detected a note of approval in Bradshaw's voice. Maybe the sheriff was even a little impressed. And maybe, just maybe, when all this was over, the marijuana-plot stakeout fiasco would be forgotten.

18

IT WAS LATE afternoon as Rivera pulled up to the curb in front of the Vance residence in Vernal and stepped out of his vehicle into the autumn chill. There was a faint smell of burning leaves in the air. The Vance house was a small, colonial-style home surrounded by a green lawn and several gardens with autumn flowers in bloom. Large cottonwood trees now showing hints of gold shaded the house from the afternoon sun. He proceeded up the flagstone walkway to the front door. The doorbell produced a pleasant chord of chimes.

The Vances invited him inside. Rivera sat down on a comfortable beige couch in the living room while Kenneth Vance, a tall slender man with only a few wisps of white hair remaining on his head, sat down on a stuffed chair across from him. The older man wore wire-rimmed glasses, a red plaid shirt, and blue twill trousers.

Rivera glanced around the room. The furniture was predominately early 20th century antiques. At the far end of the living room was a baby grand piano, on top of which sat a vase with freshly-cut yellow flowers.

"Thanks for seeing me on such short notice," said Rivera.

"Would you like some iced tea?" asked Jill Vance. She was a plumpish woman with short auburn hair and a pretty face.

"Yes ma'am. Thank you very much." He was thirsty after the 4-hour drive across the mountains.

She retrieved a pitcher from the kitchen, poured him a glass, and added a wedge of lemon. She sat down on the far end of the couch.

Rivera leaned back on the soft cushions and took a swallow. He briefly considered the Vances. They seemed like a happy couple, the kind who had grown together over the years. They were cordial and courteous, but he noted a slight look of apprehension on their faces. Not wanting his hosts to feel uncomfortable about the as-yet-unstated purpose of his visit, he got right to the point.

"It's possible that some old letters, written to Rebecca Ann Cross back in the 1930s, might contain information that could possibly shed some light on an investigation I'm conducting. It seems that . . ."

"Well, I'll be darned," interrupted Kenneth Vance who turned and looked at his wife. Both faces bore expressions of astonishment. Rivera waited. "It wasn't more than two months ago that a fellow came here looking for old letters. He said he was a graduate student at the University of Utah and was helping a professor who was compiling a history of the effects of the depression on the Four Corners area. He said the professor was specifically looking for older letters that reflected life in this area in the 1930s. He said the work was being conducted under a government grant and there was money available for any useful historical information."

Rivera extracted Sorenson's university photograph from a manila folder. "Is this the man?"

Kenneth Vance adjusted his glasses and peered at the photo. "Yes Sir, that's him."

"Did you sell him the letters?"

"No. Well, not at first. I knew we had some old family photographs and correspondence up in the attic that belonged to my mother, Ruth Cross Vance. Two large cardboard boxes full. And one small box, a shoe box, that belonged to her sister. That would be Rebecca Ann Cross, my Aunt Becky. We asked the man to wait while we went into the kitchen and discussed it privately. We weren't sure why we were selected for this, but finally decided it couldn't do any harm and we could sure use some extra money. We live on my small pension and our social security income. So we took him up into the attic where he looked through the contents of the boxes. Then he offered us five hundred dollars for the letters in the small box, my Aunt Becky's old letters.

I thought that was a real fine offer and asked him if he had any interest in the stuff in the large boxes, my mother's letters and memorabilia. He said no, just the small box. I told him we'd like to think about it and asked him if he could come back the next day."

Rivera sipped on his iced tea and listened attentively, his spirits slowly sinking at the thought of the letters having been sold.

"The wife and I talked it over that night. We didn't exactly feel right about selling the letters. After all, they did belong to Aunt Becky. But we also figured she'd probably forgotten about them by now and wouldn't ever ask for them. She's very old and doesn't do much anymore. Just sits in her room. Seems to have lost the desire to talk to anyone. Then we discussed the money. It was a lot to pay for a bunch of old letters. We wondered if maybe he was really after the stamps. Maybe they had some value. So we decided if we sold the letters, we would keep the envelopes. Then we talked about the letters some more. They were Aunt Becky's personal property and we really had no right to sell them. In the end, we decided that since they may have useful historical information, we'd be willing to make photocopies of the letters and sell him those. We weren't sure copies would be acceptable but we figured, for purely information content, they would be as good as the originals."

"Did he return the next day?" asked Rivera.

"He came the next afternoon and said copies would be fine. So we went to the local stationery store with him and made a copy of each letter. He paid us five hundred dollars in cash, took the copies, and left."

Rivera's inhaled deeply. "And do you still have the originals?" he asked.

"We sure do. They're up in the attic back in that same shoebox."

"I would like to take them with me as possible evidence in a homicide case. They would of course be returned."

"A homicide case?"

"Yes. I can't go into the details now but I assure you this is important. And time is of the essence."

After some further discussion, Kenneth Vance left the room shaking his head and went up to the attic. While he was gone, Rivera asked Jill Vance what she knew about Becky's history. "Kenneth's mother Ruth, she was Becky's older sister, told me a lot about her. Becky and Ruth lived with their mother in Colorado Springs. They were both schoolteachers. Becky was engaged to be married to a ranch hand named Liam Scott who lived in Moab. But Liam wanted to wait to marry Becky until he could provide her with a good home. They were both saving their money so they could buy a small ranch and start their life together. When Liam suddenly disappeared from her life, she was very upset. After a few months went by, she became distant and despondent. She had no way of knowing what had happened to him or even if he was still alive. They contacted Liam's ranch foreman but he was just as mystified as we were. He had no idea what had become of Liam. Neither did the sheriff. Ruth said their mother told Becky she was still young and attractive and wouldn't have any trouble finding someone else. But Becky just became more introspective and reclusive. She quit her teaching job and from then on only chose jobs that didn't involve a lot of contact with people. She never met another man who interested her, and never really looked for one. In 1946, her mother died of cancer, which was another blow to Becky. She continued living in the family home in Colorado Springs, and over the years, became more and more withdrawn. Eventually, she seemed to prefer living within her own thoughts and stopped talking. When that happened, Ruth and her husband Thomas took her into their home here in Vernal. Ruth sold the family home in Colorado Springs but kept most of the furniture. That's the furniture you see in this room. The substantial collection of books in the house was sold to a used book dealer here in Vernal. Ruth kept the personal papers and family memorabilia and when she passed away, we stored them in our attic."

Jill Vance took a sip of iced tea. "Anyway, by 1985, Ruth and Thomas were no longer able to give Becky the care she needed due to their own advancing years. So they moved Becky to The Cenizo Home for the Elderly here in Vernal, not far from their home. They visited her every week, and made sure she didn't want for anything. By 1996, both Ruth and Thomas had passed away, so Kenny and I assumed the duty of looking after Becky. Now, she spends most of her time in her room just staring out the window."

"Yes. I spoke to the director of the home. He said pretty much the same thing."

"How did you learn about the letters?" she asked.

"We found some old diaries written by Becky when she was young. They were purchased from a used book store here in Vernal. The diaries made reference to the letters she had received from Liam."

"Oh dear, I'd forgotten all about those. Ruth told me that Becky started keeping a diary when she was ten years old. She said Becky was very faithful about making daily entries. The diaries must have been in the boxes of books that Ruth sold to that book dealer when she cleaned out the Colorado Springs house." She paused. "I wonder if we could get those back. I'm sure Ruth never meant to sell them."

"I'll see what I can do about that," said Rivera.

Kenneth Vance returned from the attic with the old shoebox of letters addressed to Rebecca Ann Cross. "I don't understand any of this but we absolutely must get these back," he said, as he presented the box to the deputy.

Rivera reassured him they would be returned and wrote out a hand receipt.

"Can you tell us anything at all about how these old letters are connected to a homicide?"

"I'm afraid not but I promise to call you and fill you in after we break the case."

Rivera departed the Vance residence and drove to a local diner. After he had ordered coffee and a tuna salad sandwich, he opened the box. Inside were three faded photographs. He studied them for a moment, and then set them aside. His primary interest was the letters. He decided to start by reading the last letter and working his way back in time.

July 21, 1938

Dear Becky,

Some very bad news. Josh has gotten much sicker over the past few weeks. About ten days ago he told me he was dying of cancer. He said I was his best friend and he was leaving his secret cave and its contents to me. He also said he was leaving his Castle Valley cabin to Juan Medina, his old friend from Cortez. Josh was in a lot of pain. The doc here gave him some morphine pills, but I don't think they were helping much.

Then, three days ago, Josh took his own life. He shot himself in the temple. I miss him a lot but at least he's not suffering anymore. There was a big funeral in Moab yesterday.

Everybody around town came. Then, that evening, Juan and I buried Josh in his orchard.

Becky, the pots in the cave now make me a man of means. So I have a lot of thinking to do. I will write again soon.

Love,
Liam

Rivera thought about the last paragraph for a moment. Those were the last words Becky ever heard from him. What did he mean about having a lot of thinking to do? About the pots in the cave? Or about his relationship with Becky? No wonder she became withdrawn after he disappeared. He continued reading the letters, going backward in time. There was a letter from Liam every week or two.

Soon, he reached a letter dated May 23, 1938. It contained the information he'd been hoping for:

May 23, 1938

Dearest Becky,

A most interesting thing has just happened. My friend Josh Cummings took me on one of his adventures last weekend. It was all very mysterious. He wouldn't tell me where we were going. He said it was a surprise. We left his place in Castle Valley early Saturday morning and rode our horses upriver to Onion Creek. There we followed the creek through some of the most beautiful canyon country I've ever seen. I hope someday to show it to you. We ascended from the canyon, crossed Fisher Valley, and left our horses there. We descended Cottonwood Canyon on foot. We talked about you a lot. After a long ways, we turned up a side canyon that Josh called Burro Canyon. We were trespassing on private land so the whole operation was filled with danger and suspense. Josh said we were on Rutherford Ranch property. About a hundred yards up the side canyon, we climbed up a rocky slope to a narrow terrace at the base of the towering cliff. It looked to me like we were going nowhere until Josh disappeared through a crack behind a large slab of fallen cap rock leaning against the face of the cliff. Behind the slab was Josh's secret cave and it was full of old Indian pots and figurines. Josh told me all about them and how he'd traded for them over the past fifty years. He said they'd become very valuable.

I asked him how in the world he'd found the cave. He said a Ute elder he used to trade with told him about the cave a few months before he died. That was around the turn of the century. The Indian said he'd found it one day while hunting mule deer and that he was the only one who knew about it. Josh has been using it ever since.

I asked him why all those Indian pots were in there. He said he began storing them there about thirty years ago. He said he was what you might call a collector. As a trader, he was gone for weeks or months at a time, so he couldn't leave them at home—they might've gotten stolen. He said that he always loved Indian pottery, that each piece is a one-of-a-kind work of art. Whenever he got a good one in trade, he'd bring it to the cave for safe-keeping.

Then he said he just wanted me to know where the place was and that it was a big secret, so please don't mention it to anyone. I know I can trust you.

Other than this adventure with Josh, there's not much new since the last time I wrote you. Things are pretty slow at the ranch. We drove the herd up into the mountains to graze on the fresh grass, so now we're mostly just repairing things around the ranch. Josh said to tell you hello. I'm worried about him. He's been sick lately and doesn't look so good. But he's indestructible so I'm sure he'll get well.

I miss you greatly and look forward to seeing you again soon.

All my love always,
Liam

Rivera folded up the letter and put it back in its envelope. So there it was, he thought. The cave was in Burro Canyon, close to where he'd found the shell casing and the second potsherd. He had yet to see exactly how this related to Montoya's murder, but a connection now seemed certain.

On a hunch, he called his friend Christopher Carey in Moab. Now retired, Carey was a journalist who spent his career working for various Utah newspapers, including the Moab *Times-Independent*. He asked Carey if he would search the Moab newspaper archives for any information related to Josh Cummings or Liam Scott in the 1930s timeframe. Rivera said he was working on a case where the information might be helpful. Carey said he was slightly bored in retirement and jumped at the chance to help. He said he'd call Rivera back as soon as he had something.

Rivera decided to return to Moab, get a good night's sleep, and head for Burro Canyon in the morning. He would find that cave and see what was in it.

19

SORENSON SITUATED HIMSELF in the usual spot atop the bluff overlooking Cedar Mesa. It was a warm afternoon with a gentle breeze. He took a drink of water and settled into a comfortable position. Adjusting the focus of his binoculars, he surveyed the expanse below, looking for a plume of dust in the distance that would signal the approach of Twitchell's vehicle. He saw no activity. While he waited, he scanned the horizon. Some 80 miles to the southwest, just beyond Navajo Mountain, was a large thunderhead, bright white on top and black underneath, with fingers of lightning flashing in the darkness. The Navajos on that part of the reservation would be grateful. The rest of the horizon was bathed in sunlight. To the south, some 40 miles distant, he could see the buttes and spires of Monument Valley. To the east rose the Abajo Mountains.

He put down the binoculars and leaned back against the rock that had become so familiar to him. As he waited, he began thinking about his life and how much it had changed since he'd been discharged from the Army and began looking for work. There weren't a lot of job opportunities for ex-snipers. Eventually he found work with an insurance agency in Tucson, selling whole life policies to retired military. That job lasted nine years. After that, he worked as a salesman for four years in a wholesale lumberyard. Then came three years of selling automobiles at a used car dealership in Phoenix. He'd found each one of these jobs incredibly boring but he needed to make a living.

The cry of a raven intruded on his thoughts. He raised his binoculars and watched the graceful bird soar and glide on currents of air. He turned his binoculars southward and surveyed the mesa. Still no sign of a vehicle. He looked at his watch. Another twenty minutes to go before Twitchell was scheduled to arrive. He was never late and never early. Always right on time. Sorenson liked that about him. He put down the binoculars, leaned back against the rock, and resumed his reflections.

He'd always believed his run of boring jobs would one day come to an end. He smiled as he remembered the moment his life took a turn for the better. Sitting in his dentist's waiting room, he'd picked up an old copy of *National Geographic*. As he flipped through the pages absently looking for something to read, a photograph of old Indian arrowheads and spear tips caught his attention. The accompanying article described an archaeological dig in the Four Corners area, the artifacts which had been uncovered, and the anthropological theories and conclusions advanced by experts who studied such matters. He was intrigued by how much the scientists were able to infer about how those early societies functioned.

He'd read the article in its entirety and became fascinated by the work and its challenges. He wondered what his life would have been like if he'd pursued archaeology or anthropology while he was young. Working outdoors and exploring for clues to the past, then performing research in a modern laboratory—what could be better? And why couldn't he be doing that for a living instead of selling cars? He remembered a warmth slowly engulfing him as he sat there. It was part epiphany and part inspiration. He was never one to shy away from a challenge, and the idea of returning to school after so many years rejuvenated him. It had the potential to make his life interesting again. So, sitting there, that day, he'd decided to enroll in school and begin studying for a degree in anthropology.

Starting life over at 53 years of age had been exhilarating. Using his G.I. Bill benefits, he'd enrolled at the University of Utah to pursue a degree in anthropology. He did well in school, loved the university life, and dedicated himself to his studies. He completed his Bachelor's degree in three years, graduated with honors, and began working on his Master's degree. His life had turned around. He was happy again, a feeling he hadn't had since his days in the Army.

Working on a Master's degree had made him feel even better about himself. Proud, in fact. And getting the job last year as a student assistant helping the history professor with his research was a real stroke of good fortune. It was the beginning of a sequence of events that led him to Josh's secret cave.

Sorenson enjoyed replaying in his mind what had happened: The professor specialized in the history of southeast Utah during the nineteenth and early-twentieth centuries. Part of Sorenson's job involved going to auctions to buy collections of old history books, mainly from estate sales and wholesale dealers. Sorenson would separate out the books related to the history of Utah, many old and out of print, and resell the unrelated ones at auction. In this way the professor could accumulate old books, records, and journals at practically no cost. In addition to books, the estate sales and auctions sometimes produced photos, family records, and diaries of everyday people that were also useful in assembling a detailed historical picture. The net result was a unique source of information that the professor could use to support his voracious appetite for producing peer-reviewed articles. The search for items of historical value was slow and the yield of quality items low, but the occasional gem made the process worthwhile. And besides, the cost of a student assistant's time was only slightly above a serf's wages. But sometimes a serf gets lucky.

Sorenson recalled the day he came across the set of fifteen diaries which would launch him on the journey of a lifetime. The diaries had been part of a larger collection of used books which were being sold by a small bookstore in Vernal, Utah, during a going-out-of-business sale. The professor had read a small item in the classified advertising section of the *Salt Lake Tribune* and dispatched Sorenson to "Get over there early and find the best stuff. And this time don't come back with a bunch of useless junk we'll just have to re-sell." Sorenson grinned as he thought about what had happened. The professor, one Harold B. Jenkins, PhD., treated him like dirt. He was inconsiderate, abrupt, and disrespectful. But this time, Sorenson had gotten the best of his boss. And he was determined to convert this opportunity into his own personal gain.

He'd gone to Vernal early that day, waited for the store to open, and was the first customer to enter. The store was actually an old house located a few blocks from the center of town, with each room dedicated to a different category of books. The former kitchen contained books on cooking, the dining room was devoted to fiction, and so forth. After a short search, Sorenson found a section called Utah Geology, Ranching, History, and Anthropology located in a back bedroom. As he thought about that old house where his good fortune had begun, he could still smell the musty odor of old books and feel the excitement at the start of a new search. As much as he disliked the caustic professor, he loved the thrill of the hunt, even if it was just for old books. He filled 26 cardboard boxes with items he thought appropriate to the subject of Utah history. The cost was only $20 per box, so Sorenson took everything he thought even remotely pertinent. He paid the dealer, loaded the merchandise into his pickup truck, and drove back to the University, arriving late that evening. He carried the boxes to his office and went home.

The following day he returned to the office and began the process of sorting and cataloging. By mid-morning, the unpacking and stacking had left him with an aching lower back so he decided to take a break. The last box he'd opened contained, among other things, a set of old diaries. He sat in his chair and read them as a diversion while he rested. Feeling a bit like a voyeur, but enjoying himself nonetheless, he came upon the volume where the romance between Liam and Becky was unfolding. In time, he reached the entries which described Josh and the secret cave loaded with pots and figurines. Was it possible the cave and its contents were still intact? Indeed it was and after a few months of clever and bold detective work, Sorenson had located the Vances and found the shoebox containing Liam's letters. And through them, he had found Josh's secret cave.

Yes, indeed. It had been a long journey from childhood to the present and now he was in the process of hitting it big financially. He looked forward to the day when he would no longer have to put up with a boss. After all the pots were sold, he would never again be anyone's employee.

If only he hadn't had to kill the ranch hand. That was the unfortunate part of all this. What would the nuns who taught him in grade school think of him now? And what on earth would his parents say? Trying to reconcile murder with his basic value system was impossible, he knew, but maybe, with the passage of time, the memory of his evil deed would just fade away.

His reflections were interrupted by the sight of a dust cloud on the horizon. He looked at his watch. It would be Twitchell, right on time as usual.

The exchange went without a hitch, Twitchell opening the box, inspecting its contents, leaving a bag of cash, and departing. After the trader was a safe distance down the road, Sorenson descended the rocks, retrieved the cash, and counted the money. He climbed back up to his vehicle, locked the bag of cash in his toolbox, and drove back to Moab. Another mission perfectly executed.

20

DONALD TWITCHELL DROVE his Jeep Rubicon into the gravel parking area behind his store in Farmington. The windowless building was a grey, concrete-block structure now tinted coral by the light of the setting sun. The front door was protected by security bars and the rear door was steel-reinforced and displayed a sign warning would-be burglars that the building was protected by the SCA Security Company. Painted high on the front of the edifice were the words *Twitchell's Indian Artifacts*. The structure was nondescript in every way, but collectors all across the country knew the man who dwelled within was an artifact guru.

Twitchell squirmed out of his vehicle, grimacing as he did. These days, his arthritis made every movement a challenge. In his late sixties and out of shape, he moved slowly. Despite his physical limitations, he loved the challenge and intrigue of the artifacts business and looked forward to coming to work each day. It was his whole life. He walked to the rear door, unlocked it, and held it open. He slid a yellow rock over with his foot to keep it open. He had an attachment to that rock. More like an affection. He'd been using it as a doorstop for over forty years. He'd miss it if it were ever taken by someone, but it was unlikely anyone but him ever noticed it. He returned to the passenger side of his SUV, opened the door, and lifted out the cardboard box resting on the floor. A gentle nudge with his hip closed the vehicle door. He carried the box into the back room of the store and placed it on one of the workbenches. He returned to the rear entrance and kicked aside the rock. The door swung closed, the tell-tale click indicating it was now locked.

Twitchell shuffled back to the workbench, sat down on a grey metal stool, and opened the box. One by one, he carefully lifted out the three artifacts and placed them on the bench. He gently removed the protective bubble-wrap from each. He turned on the gooseneck lamp clamped to the edge of the workbench and sat back with a smile, admiring his new acquisitions. An ancient Mayan figurine, a perfect multi-colored Hopi pot made around 1910 by a well-known artist, and a large 900 year-old black-on-white Mogollon pot. What could possibly be more fun than this, he thought. And he was making a killing in the process. He laughed out loud with joy and slapped his knee.

Twitchell would prepare the provenance papers right away, and by 8:00 P.M. the items would be sold. The two buyers were expected to knock on his rear door momentarily to consummate the deal. One day's work and a $16,000 profit. As he always did when filling out the bogus documents, he would cite various locations on his small ranches in southwest Colorado and southeast Arizona as the discovery sites. This deception protected his buyers from being prosecuted for violating the Antiquities Act. If challenged, they could always produce the document and claim they purchased the item in good faith, believing it was discovered on private property. Whenever Twitchell cited a particular place on one of his ranches as the source of a pot, he would take the precaution of actually going to the site and digging in the general area just in case the authorities asked to see the location of origin. He would then be able to point to the recently disturbed earth where he'd supposedly dug up the pot. A foresighted measure that cost the wily trader nothing.

He got up and went to the antique wooden desk on the other side of the room. He lowered himself into his old swivel chair, opened the center drawer and removed a manila folder. He placed it on his desk and opened it. It contained a two-page list and an envelope full of photographs. He adjusted his bifocals, ran his finger down the list, and drew a line through items #2, #17, and #41. Scanning the papers, he was pleased to see that many items still remained to be sold. That meant the fun would continue for a while longer.

Twitchell let out a grunt as he pushed himself up from the chair. He went over to the row of old grey filing cabinets lining one of the walls and pulled open a drawer. He extracted three blank provenance forms and returned to his desk. Now, how to fill these out? The buyers, who were new to him but recommended by a regular client, joked on the phone that they really didn't care about the papers—they could forge their own. But to protect himself, Twitchell would nevertheless prepare the documents and present them to the buyers. And he would make copies for his own files.

As he was filling out the forms, he heard a knock on the back door. He checked his watch. They were a few minutes early. He trudged to the rear and pushed open the door. The two men standing there smiled and introduced themselves. One was an older man, tall with broad shoulders and grey hair, wearing khaki slacks and a white shirt. The second man looked to be in his thirties, short and stocky, wearing new jeans, a yellow western-style shirt, and a tan suede jacket. They appeared friendly and eager to see the merchandise. Twitchell shook hands with them and invited them to come inside.

He led them over to his workbench where they leaned over and inspected the figurine and the two pots. Twitchell watched and awaited their reaction.

"They're beautiful," said the older man. "Perfect specimens." Twitchell beamed like a new father. The three men chatted for several minutes about the merchandise, the prices, and the market for Indian artifacts in general. They asked Twitchell where he'd gotten them. He laughed, saying he was just now filling out the provenance papers when they arrived.

"I'll say they're from my ranch properties, unless you'd rather I said something else." The three men laughed. The younger man produced a wad of cash totaling $31,000 and handed it to Twitchell.

"Thirty-one thousand dollars. That's the amount we agreed upon. Correct?"

Twitchell counted the money. "Yes, indeed. That's correct. I'll wrap the artifacts for you and finish filling out the papers."

"That won't be necessary," said the older man, producing a badge. "FBI. You're under arrest for violation of the Antiquities Act. Dealing in illegal Indian artifacts"

Twitchell stood there for a moment looking at the men in disbelief. He swallowed. Then in a low voice, he managed, "Isn't it just your word against mine?"

"My partner here is wired. This entire conversation has been recorded."

The agents placed Twitchell in handcuffs. Crestfallen, he lapsed into silence, realizing he'd failed to exercise due caution in the transaction. It occurred to him that his frequent travels to Cedar Mesa must have made him tired and careless. Or maybe it was just old age. Either way, all the fun he'd been having had just come to an end.

21

FRANK SORENSON SQUINTED at the bright red digits of the alarm clock on the end table next to his bed. It was 5:16 A.M., still over an hour before the alarm was set to go off. He was wide awake, the victim of another bad dream, the details of which had already faded from his mind. He pushed aside the covers, slid out of bed, and moved toward the window of his motel room. He pulled aside the drapes and he peered outside. Moab's Main Street was deserted except for a lone Mayflower eighteen-wheeler lumbering through town headed north. The black sky was awash with stars. A narrow band of subdued blue light across the eastern horizon outlined the barely visible peaks of the LaSal Mountains. The truck passed and downtown Moab was quiet again. He pressed the back of his hand against the window pane to judge the outside temperature. It was a chilly morning.

He considered going back to bed and resting until the alarm went off, but decided instead to get dressed and have an early breakfast. Since he now had extra time, he'd be able to go to a diner instead of cooking oatmeal and sausage in his room. A leisurely breakfast in a restaurant was a luxury he hadn't allowed himself in many days. Afterwards, he would head to the cave.

He showered, shaved off a two-day stubble, and got dressed. Today would be the last day of the five-day odyssey that had been stretched from the original three-day plan. He packed his satchel and shaving kit and left the motel room, donning his faded green cap as he shut the door behind him. He walked to his pickup truck, checked the toolbox behind the cab to ensure it hadn't been tampered with, and hopped in. The truck's engine came to life and broke the cold silence. He drove north on Main Street to the local Denny's Restaurant and pulled into the empty parking lot.

He bought a copy of Friday morning's edition of the *Salt Lake Tribune* from the vending box in front of the restaurant and entered. The place was sparsely occupied. Besides the restaurant staff, the only other occupant was an older man, probably the driver of the white tanker truck parked in front alongside the curb. It was just the way he liked it—not too many prying eyes.

He slid into a booth adjacent to a window and looked outside. The morning sky had become pale blue and reminded him of mornings in the San Rafael Swell where he often camped out in a tent for periods of up to a week, digging for Ancient-Indian artifacts in support of his thesis work. He missed that. The waitress came over to his table, greeted him, and jotted down his order for three eggs over easy, ham, hash browns, wheat toast, orange juice, and black coffee.

The coffee was served first. Sorenson took a sip from his mug and picked up the newspaper. He scanned the front page. Things in the world hadn't changed much. There was trouble in the Middle East, people being arrested for running drugs, misconduct by government officials, and corporate desecration of the environment. It all seemed so familiar. Why bother reading about it? His thoughts transitioned to his own situation. After today's trip to the cave and the subsequent exchange with Twitchell, he would rest for a couple of days before resuming his operation. He looked forward to returning to the university, if only for a little while. He loved anthropology and he loved the academic environment. He'd already made a good start on his thesis and deep down he wanted to finish it. But he felt conflicted—after all the artifacts had been sold, it would be smart to move far, far away from Burro Canyon. But that would mean leaving Utah and the university. If only he hadn't had to kill that ranch hand. Oh well, he didn't have to decide all that now. He would think about it some more later on.

Sorenson took another sip of coffee, turned the page of the newspaper, and saw the headline over the far right column on page three:

FBI ARRESTS FOUR
INDIAN ARTIFACT DEALERS
IN STING OPERATION

He sucked in a breath and quickly scanned the article for the names of the four dealers. He froze when his eyes fell on the name Donald A. Twitchell of Farmington, New Mexico.

As his mind raced through the implications of this, the waitress returned and placed his breakfast on the table. She topped off his coffee. "Will there be anything else?"

"No, thanks," he said, not looking up.

After she departed, Sorenson forced himself to settle down. He studied the article in detail. Apparently there had been a steady increase in Indian artifact prices in recent years due to high demand from wealthy collectors in the United States as well as Japan and Europe. The demand had been greater than the supply, so prices went up, making illegal trading in protected artifacts more lucrative. Dealers, traders, and collectors simply succumbed to their greed, asking few if any questions regarding true provenance, particularly for rare items of the highest quality. The FBI office in Albuquerque had been tasked by Washington to investigate and make examples of the worst offenders in an effort to stem the illicit trade. Posing as Indian artifact traders from various East and West Coast cities who would pay cash without asking too many questions, the agents had arrested four suspected offenders, Twitchell from New Mexico, and three others, two from Colorado and one from Arizona. The four sting operations had taken place simultaneously yesterday evening.

Sorenson reviewed the situation. Since he'd kept his identity hidden from Twitchell, the FBI shouldn't be able to trace the artifacts back to him. The most the trader could reveal to the FBI would be the artifact list and the photographs. Neither of these presented an immediate problem. The only other fact Twitchell could reveal was the location of the Cedar Mesa exchange point. Sorenson had been very careful to leave nothing incriminating there. Certainly he would never return.

As his mind sifted through the facts, he became less anxious. Everything was still okay. He gave himself kudos for the way he'd planned and executed the operation. He had successfully shielded his identity from Twitchell, thereby protecting himself and his merchandise.

He considered the realities of his new situation. There were now law enforcement activities at both ends of his operation. The Grand County Sheriff's Department was still investigating the shooting of Jesse Montoya, and now the FBI was investigating the man who'd been his market for the artifacts. What he needed to do now was obvious. He would continue removing items from the cave, but instead of trying to sell them, he would simply transport them to his storage unit in Blanding. There they would remain for an extended period until things cooled off. He would continue taking only three items from the cave on each trip, still posing as a lost hiker if he was ever questioned about his being on private land.

He decided to continue today's trip as planned, retrieving three more items and transferring them to his storage unit. Then he would return to Salt Lake City and deposit the cash that was stashed in his toolbox. After resting for a couple of days, he would return to Moab and resume transferring artifacts to his storage unit until the cave was empty. And the sooner, the better, he thought.

He finished breakfast, got in his truck, and drove up into the mountains. Parking in the usual place just off the Thompson Canyon Trail, he strapped on his backpack, pressed his handgun into the belt holster under his loose shirt, and began the long trek down Cottonwood Canyon. As he hiked, his mind kept sifting through the facts. Suddenly it occurred to him that with Twitchell out of the picture, he could hike from his truck to the cave and back two and possibly three times in a single day. He could leave the artifacts locked in his truck and concealed under a blanket as he went back for more. That way the cave could be emptied in less than two weeks, and the dangerous part of the operation would be over. It would be a very smart thing to do. He decided to test the new plan today by making two trips to the cave.

Sorenson felt re-energized as he descended the canyon. He looked forward to the day when he would visit the cave no more, and now that day would arrive even sooner. Not only would the remaining artifacts be secure in his storage unit, but he would no longer have to go near that skeleton in the back of the cave. He would lay low for at least a year, and then find a new buyer to replace Twitchell.

It was an unusually warm October afternoon, so Sorenson had worked up a good sweat by the time he reached Burro Canyon. He'd exercised the usual caution during the hike and had seen no one. He scampered up the talus, and squeezed into the cave. Once inside, he got right to work. He wrapped the three pots closest to him and carefully placed them in his backpack. Before departing, he peered outside the cave, cautiously looking up and down Burro Canyon. Again, no one was in sight. He left the cave, hiked back up Cottonwood Canyon to the mesa top and through the brush to his truck.

He removed his backpack and gently set it down on the ground. As he unlocked the vehicle door, he heard a rustling sound coming from the brush behind him. He pretended not to notice and slowly slipped his right hand under his shirt and onto his revolver. Then in a single motion, he spun around, crouched, and drew his pistol. There was a man not ten feet away, aiming a snub-nose revolver in his direction. He felt a sharp pain in his chest, then everything faded to black and he felt nothing.

22

MANNY RIVERA HAD planned to sleep until 8:00 A.M. on Friday morning because of his late return from Vernal the night before. But at 6:15 A.M., he was jolted out of bed by the sound of a ringing telephone.

"Hello."

"Manny, it's Chris Carey. Sorry to call you so early but I'm leaving town in a little while for some elk hunting."

"Hi, Chris. That's Okay."

"I did some research last night in the *Times-Independent* archives. I found several articles that mentioned Josh Cummings. He was a trader from the Moab area who helped pioneer the Four Corners area from around 1890 up until 1938 when he died. In his early years, he operated down around the Utah-Arizona border. He helped John Wetherill explore the uncharted canyon country between Monument Valley and Navajo Mountain. He also helped him establish trading posts at Oljeto and Kayenta. Evidently he was a very popular guy around Moab. Good reputation and lots of friends. He lived in a cabin in Castle Valley on a five-acre tract. One article said he was rumored to have a large collection of Indian pots and that he'd gotten many of them from Wetherill—either bought or traded for. But no one ever saw the collection. And after he died, the pots weren't found among his belongings. So no one was ever sure it really existed. That's about all I could find on Cummings."

"That's actually very helpful," said Rivera. "What about Liam Scott?"

"Only two references to Scott. He's mentioned as a pallbearer in Josh Cummings's funeral. He's also the subject of a missing persons report filed by his ranch foreman with the Sheriff's Office. I couldn't find anything else on him. I made copies of the articles for you. I'll have my wife drop them by your office later today."

"Thanks a lot, Chris. That helps fill out a picture I've been trying to piece together. And good luck on the hunt."

Rivera's plan for the day was to meet Emmett Mitchell for breakfast at the diner, then drive across the Castleton-Gateway Road to Burro Canyon and search for the cave. The pieces of the puzzle were starting to fit together, and he looked forward to bouncing his theories off Mitchell. There was still no sign of Sorenson, but perhaps the state-wide APB he put out would produce some results.

As Rivera entered the diner, he saw Mitchell sitting at the usual booth in the far corner, warming his hands on a mug of steaming coffee. Rivera sat down across from him just as Betty arrived at the table.

"Good morning, handsome," she said as she deposited a mug of hot coffee in front of Rivera. As usual, she was smiling at him and chewing gum.

"Hi, Betty," he grinned. "Thanks." As he took a sip, he looked at Mitchell over the rim of the mug, wanting to start telling his story, but waiting because Betty was still standing there.

"You boys want the usual today?" she asked. Both men nodded. She scratched the order on her pad in that shorthand waitresses use, and departed to pass the information on to the cook.

"Emmett, I've got a lot to tell you," Rivera said in a low voice, and proceeded to bring Mitchell up-to-date. He recapped what had happened up until the time of his trip to the university. Then he related everything he'd learned during his visit to Salt Lake City. He told Mitchell about his visit with Professor Hollingsworth, the reconstructed pot with two missing pieces in the ceramics lab, and the fact that the two sherds he'd brought with him were a perfect fit for the voids. He covered his search of Sorenson's office, the contents of the desk, the diaries from 1938, and his trip to Vernal. Finally, he summarized the contents of Liam's letters. Mitchell appeared spellbound as he listened with wide-eyed interest. Rivera concluded by saying he was going to search for the cave today.

"Wow. That's quite a story. It sounds like a great script for a movie. I wish I could go with you and help in the search."

"You'd be most welcome."

"Unfortunately, Burro Canyon is outside my jurisdiction. And besides, I have to be in court in Monticello all day. Lately, your job seems a lot more interesting than mine."

Betty returned to the table with their breakfast orders and refilled their coffee mugs. Mitchell was the first to speak after she departed. "So the killing may not have been about drugs after all. It may have been about Indian artifacts." It was a statement, not a question.

"That's the conclusion I've been coming around to. But I can't completely rule out a dope deal gone bad. Montoya was a known user. And his true identity is still clouded in mystery."

Mitchell nodded and then raised a new subject. "By the way, did you hear about the FBI's sting operation last night?"

He hadn't, and so Mitchell filled him in. When Mitchell finished the story, he said exactly what Rivera was thinking. "I wonder if the two cases are somehow related."

Later that morning, Rivera was driving on the Castleton-Gateway Road across the LaSal Mountains toward the Rutherford ranch. As a courtesy, he planned to invite Paul Williamson to join in the search for the cave. If Liam's letter was correct, the cave would be on Rutherford Ranch property. Also, Rivera wouldn't mind having a little help exploring for the opening to the cave. Williamson knew those canyons a lot better than he did. If the foreman wasn't available, he would, of course, perform the search alone.

Rivera's cell phone rang. It was Millie Ives.

"Manny, we just got a call from two boys who were riding their ATVs down the Thompson Canyon Trail. They said they'd found a man alongside the trail, apparently shot in the chest. They said it looked pretty bad. They weren't sure if he was alive. Said they didn't know what to do. They sounded young and pretty shook up."

"Millie, I'm not far from there. Maybe ten minutes away. Headed there now."

"I've called MedEvac. Their chopper is over in Grand Junction. They're rerouting to an open meadow near the intersection of the Thompson Canyon Trail and the Castleton-Gateway Road."

"OK, Millie. I'll report back as soon as I get to the scene."

Rivera turned left at the Thompson Canyon Trail and drove a little too fast down the rocky trail. Minutes later, he spotted a red pickup truck on the right side of the road. Two young boys were huddled next to their ATVs on the left side. He grabbed his first aid kit, jumped out of his truck, and ran over to the body lying on the ground. He recognized Frank Sorenson immediately from his university photograph.

"We weren't sure if he was dead or not," said one of the boys in a nervous voice. "We didn't know what to do."

Rivera felt for a pulse. "He's alive. You may have saved his life by calling for help."

Rivera pressed a couple of buttons on his cell phone dialing the dispatcher's stored phone number. He told Millie the victim was still alive and medical help was needed ASAP. Then he turned his attention to Sorenson. The bullet had struck him on the left side of his chest. It didn't look good, thought Rivera, but if the chopper got here soon enough, there was a chance the man could be saved. He carefully washed the entry wound using alcohol from a plastic bottle. He noted that there wasn't a great deal of bleeding. Then, he applied a large wad of gauze as a compress for the wound.

Sorenson's eyes opened partially. He coughed and slowly became conscious. "What . . . happened?" he asked in a strained gravelly voice.

"You were shot. A MedEvac helicopter is on the way. The bullet is probably lodged in your chest, so try not to move."

He blinked his eyes. "I don't feel much of anything."

"Just try to relax. And don't talk."

But Sorenson was becoming fully conscious and apparently wanted to talk. "Look," he said, "I spent a lot of years in the Army. Saw lots of guys get shot. I know what it means when you get a chest wound and don't feel much pain."

Looking at Sorenson's ashen face, Rivera figured he was probably right. "Who did this?" he asked.

"I don't know. Some guy just walked up and shot me." He coughed again. "Never saw him before." He tried to raise his head but couldn't. He turned his eyes toward his pickup. "There was a lot of cash in my toolbox. Maybe somehow he found out about it, but I don't see how."

Rivera told Sorenson he'd been looking for him for the past couple of days.

Sorenson squinted his eyes and took a long look at Rivera. "Why were you looking for me?"

With nothing to do but wait for the chopper, Rivera spent several minutes telling Sorenson the whole story. He started with finding the body, then talked about the potsherds and the shell casing, and finished by describing his trip to the University and the discovery of the reconstructed pot in the ceramics lab. "I searched your office at the university. Found Becky's diaries." Rivera paused. "I went to Vernal and found Liam's letters, same as you did." Sorenson managed a grim smile as he listened. He looked at Rivera with an expression that seemed to reflect both admiration and respect. Rivera concluded by saying, "You did some real good detective work finding the cave."

"You did some real good detective work figuring everything out," replied Sorenson in a weak voice.

"I was on my way to Burro Canyon today to find the cave. Then I got a call about you," said Rivera.

Sorenson was quiet for a moment, apparently in thought. "I should have thrown those potsherds away instead of hiring Dennis to reconstruct the pot. Big mistake."

"Your big mistake was shooting that ranch hand."

"Yeah. That's something I regret," he said, sounding forlorn and making no attempt at a denial. "That's not the way I was raised." He coughed and a trickle of blood flowed from the corner of his mouth.

"How come he was shot in the top of the head?"

"He was bending over looking at the pots when I shot him. He fell on one of them. Shattered it. That's the pot I asked Dennis to reconstruct."

Rivera glanced at his watch. It would be at least another ten minutes before the chopper arrived. He wished he could do more for Sorenson.

After a long silence, Rivera spoke. "How do you feel?" he asked.

"I feel . . . ashamed," replied Sorenson, not answering the intended question. His speech was slurred but he managed to get the words out. "This is not the way

I wanted to end up. I wanted to be a teacher, a professor. Someone people looked up to. I was happy. Finally found what I wanted to do in life. And now this." He paused, as if reflecting. "I wish I'd never found Liam's letters."

The minutes ticked by. Finally, Rivera heard the thump-thump of helicopter blades in the distance. The sound became louder as the craft neared the landing site. Maybe Sorenson would make it after all, he thought.

"There's still one thing I don't understand," said Rivera. "After you shot Montoya, why did you move his body all the way up Cottonwood Canyon to the Kokopelli Trail?"

Sorenson, his breathing becoming increasingly labored, looked perplexed. He struggled to speak. "Move the body? I didn't move the body." He coughed several times and more blood trickled from his mouth. Then Rivera felt his body go limp. He checked for a pulse and found none. Sorenson was gone.

23

IT WAS MID-MORNING on Saturday as Rivera drove east across the LaSal Mountains on the Castleton-Gateway Road, intending to finally accomplish the task he'd set out to do yesterday—namely, find the cave. He would first stop by the Rutherford Ranch to see if Paul Williamson was available to assist in the search.

The crime scene investigation yesterday had consumed the entire afternoon and evening. Dr. Pudge Devlin had arrived and pronounced Sorenson officially dead, and the MedEvac team had removed the body. Adam Dunne, the BLM investigative officer arrived later and assisted Rivera in securing the crime scene and gathering evidence. The investigation had yielded several important facts.

First, the steel toolbox welded behind the cab of Sorenson's pickup had been pried open, apparently with a tire tool. The contents had been removed. The tire tool was nowhere to be found. Second, Sorenson's unopened backpack contained three carefully wrapped Indian artifacts. Third, the glove box of the truck contained a stack of fifty-four artifact photographs held together with a rubber band and a copy of the two-page list Rivera found in Sorenson's desk. Last, a set of size-eleven boot prints led up the Thompson Canyon Trail three hundred yards to a place where a vehicle had been parked. The man had been running. Casts of the boot prints and tire-tread impressions were made.

After the crime scene investigation had been completed, Rivera had returned to the office and gone over all the details with Sheriff Bradshaw. Bradshaw remained calm and professional during the briefing and asked all the right questions. Then he uncharacteristically lost his composure.

"What in the hell is going on out there?" Bradshaw had asked rhetorically. "We haven't had a murder in the backcountry in thirty years. Now suddenly we get two in one week." He rose from his chair and started pacing back and forth. "So a murderer is killed. No big deal. It's not like we lost a good citizen. But now the community will be going berserk because the damn tourist season is jeopardized. Sorenson's murder will be page-one headlines in all of Utah's newspapers tomorrow. It'll be the lead story in tonight's news broadcasts. And there'll be a rehashing of the Montoya killing." He walked over to the window and looked outside, standing there, as if trying to calm himself down. "We got the bad guy and now there's a new killer loose in the backcountry."

As Rivera had left the sheriff's office, he had a feeling of déjà vu. He'd just been assigned the job of finding Sorenson's killer and had no idea where to start.

He rolled down the window of his truck and breathed in the fresh mountain air. The aspens, now mostly golden, seemed to be filled with raucous birds celebrating the new day. He expected to arrive at the Rutherford Ranch just before noon. That gave him plenty of time to think.

Sorenson had been found and freely admitted to having shot Montoya. Montoya was an innocent ranch hand who had simply been doing his job. So one mystery was solved. Sorenson had cleverly learned of the existence of the cave and was able to locate it. He was in the process of exploiting its wealth. Only about one-third of the items on the master list had been crossed off. That suggested the cave contained many more artifacts. Hopefully, Rivera would locate the cave today. But that would still leave the nagging question of why Montoya's body had been moved. And by whom.

The big question Rivera was faced with now was who had killed Sorenson. Clearly the motive was robbery; the money in the truck had been stolen. From the way Sorenson had described what had happened, the killer must have known it was there. Figuring out how he knew could well be the key to apprehending him. And how did the killer know where Sorenson parked his truck on his visits to the cave? Obviously, he'd been followed, either on the day of the murder, or on one of Sorenson's previous trips.

Rivera considered that question. Suddenly, he realized that Sorenson must have been followed on a previous day. If he'd been followed yesterday, the day of the shooting, the money would have been removed from the truck while Sorenson was in the canyon hiking to the cave. There would have been no need for a shooting. That made the question a rather simple one. Who knew enough about what was going on in Sorenson's life to have known to follow him in the first place? Could it have been someone from the university? Only the provost, Professor Hollingsworth, and the two laboratory technicians knew about the reconstructed pot and the missing pieces. Any one of them could have followed Sorenson. But that had to be wrong. They had no idea of the existence of the cave and the other artifacts. As far as they knew, there was only one pot.

Rivera stopped his pickup on a grassy overlook some two-thousand feet above Fisher Valley. He opened the door, grabbed his coffee cup, and got out. He walked over to the edge of the cliff and sat down on a block of basalt rock. He sipped his coffee and stared down at the valley. From where he sat, he could almost see the place where Montoya's body had been found. Surely the Vances weren't involved in this. They had met Sorenson when he came in search of Liam's letters. It was possible that, after the transaction, they had read the letters themselves and had become suspicious of Sorenson's true motives. After all, he had only been interested in the contents of Becky's shoebox and didn't even consider the larger boxes containing the personal records of Ruth, Becky's sister. That must have struck them as odd. The Vance's were probably physically unable to track Sorenson themselves, but they could have gotten someone to do it for them, perhaps a son or a nephew. Rivera shook his head, made a wry face. That theory just didn't seem consistent with the quality couple he had met in Vernal. He felt a sense of grasping at straws.

A black butterfly with bright blue markings landed on his shoe, rested there a moment, then flew off. Rivera took another sip of coffee. So who else could have known Sorenson was coming into a lot of money? And who could have known that a great deal of it was stashed in his pickup truck? There was no evidence to suggest that Sorenson had a partner. All the bank accounts were in his name only. That forced Rivera's thinking to the buyer of the merchandise. Did the buyer have a reason for wanting Sorenson dead? Had Sorenson double-crossed or cheated the buyer somehow? Rivera pondered that for a moment. It didn't seem likely for three reasons. First, it looked like Sorenson's plan had been moving ahead with a clockwork precision. He was simply going to the cave, collecting merchandise, and selling it. Each trip produced a handsome sum of money. So the buyer must have been satisfied with the arrangement. Sorenson seemed to be holding up his end of the deal. Also, if the killer had been the buyer, he'd have had enough sense to check Sorenson's backpack for merchandise. He'd have recognized the value of its contents and would have taken the three pots in addition to the cash. And lastly, Sorenson said he'd never before seen the man who shot him. Surely he knew what his buyer looked like.

Rivera got back into his truck, having decided that his next step in the Sorenson murder case would be to talk with prominent artifact collectors in the Four Corners area. One of them might be able to help him identify Sorenson's buyer. From there, he might be able to develop a list of people who knew what Sorenson was up to. As he pulled back onto the gravel of the Castleton-Gateway Road, he wished he'd asked Sorenson who his buyer was. Too late now.

One step at a time, Rivera reminded himself. And the next step was to find the cave.

He arrived at the Rutherford ranch house around noon, spoke to Sarah Williamson, and learned that her husband Paul was at the ranch today. She said he rode out to the north pastures early in the morning to check on the routing of some new cross-fencing the hands were about to build. "I expect him back here shortly for lunch, though," she added. Rivera told her he was going to Burro Canyon to do some searching and wondered if Paul might like to join him there and lend a hand. He didn't elaborate. "I'll let him know your plans as soon as he returns," Sarah assured him. "I'm sure he'll want to do whatever he can to help you."

Rivera left the ranch house and drove across the pastures into the mouth of Cottonwood Canyon. He navigated his vehicle up the rough road, finally reaching Burro Canyon. He stopped the truck, stepped out and closed the door. He shaded his eyes and surveyed the area. Everything looked the same as it did the last time he was here, but now he had a new interest in the talus slopes leading up to the cliff faces. From his shirt pocket, he extracted a photocopy of Liam's letter dated May 23, 1938. He stood next to his vehicle and reread it.

24

DEXTER MIGGS AIMED the beam of his flashlight from place to place, trying to make sense of what he was seeing. Inside the cave was a bewildering array of ancient Indian artifacts. He quickly reached a conclusion. This must be what Twitchell was buying from the guy Miggs had been tracking. This was what was in the boxes that Twitchell had been picking up on Cedar Mesa.

He spotted the propane lantern, ignited it, and switched off his flashlight. He sat down on the floor of the cave and began sorting through the facts.

Twitchell had hired him to track a man and report back on all his movements and activities. He was never to make contact with the man or be seen by him. The fee was $10,000 for ten days of surveillance. The old trader had said he had a business arrangement with the man which was entirely satisfactory and which he did not wish to see disrupted. He just wanted to satisfy his curiosity about the man on the other end of the transaction: who he was, what he did, where he went, and who he spoke with. Miggs wasn't sure he believed the curiosity motive, but it didn't matter to him. His interest was in doing the job and collecting his fee.

Twitchell had told him about the rendezvous point on Cedar Mesa and what took place there. On certain days, a paper bag would be swapped for a cardboard box. No details were given about the contents of either. The trader had given Miggs the GPS coordinates of the exchange point.

A swap had been scheduled for 2:00 P.M. four days ago. Miggs remembered arriving atop the bluff early that morning to locate a position with an advantageous viewpoint. Using his GPS receiver, he drove on the dirt road a half-mile past the exchange point and parked his pickup well off the road in a thicket of junipers. Then he hiked straight to the edge of the bluff. He found a place where his line of sight from the brush that concealed him permitted a clear view of the exchange point. His small backpack contained water, snacks, high-power binoculars, a digital camera with a telephoto lens, and a radio-frequency tracking device.

He'd waited and watched. Around noon, a man in a red pickup truck arrived below at the exchange point. He deposited a cardboard box behind a large rock and left. An hour later, his truck appeared at the top of the bluff. The driver walked to the edge of the bluff, sat down, and began scanning the mesa below with his binoculars. Both activities had been documented with photographs.

At 2:00 P.M., Twitchell had arrived down below in his Rubicon. He got out and made his way through the brush to the box. He opened the box and inspected the contents. Then he closed the box and carried it back to his truck, leaving in its place a paper sack. Miggs took photographs but, because of the angle, was unable to see what was inside the box. After a brief moment, the Rubicon drove ahead a short distance, turned around at a wide place in the road, and then slowly departed, heading back in the direction from which it had come.

Later, Miggs had watched as the man he was to follow descended the rocks and retrieved the bag. He opened it and started counting the money it contained. Miggs took the opportunity to sprint down the dirt road to the man's pickup, attach the radio-frequency tracking device to the undercarriage, and return to his hiding place.

Minutes later, Miggs watched through his binoculars as the man climbed up the rocks, locked the paper bag in the toolbox welded behind the cab of his pickup, and drove away. The rest was easy. He'd trailed him back to his motel in Moab, following well out of sight a couple of miles behind. From the man's license plate, he was able to identify him as Frank Sorenson of Salt Lake City.

The next day, he followed the radio signals from the tracking device to the Thompson Canyon Trail where Sorenson had parked his vehicle. From there, he followed Sorenson's footprints over to Cottonwood Canyon where he turned right and descended the canyon. Miggs had gone part way down the canyon and then waited in the brush of a side arroyo for Sorenson's return. Hours later and some thirty minutes after Sorenson passed the arroyo headed back up the canyon, Miggs descended the canyon, following Sorenson's fresh footprints to see where he'd gone. He wanted his report to Twitchell to be complete in every detail. It was just the way he did things. His reputation as a competent sleuth meant a great deal to him, especially now that he'd left his life of crime and gone straight.

He'd followed the footprints to Burro Canyon where they turned right and headed up the side canyon. At that point, he decided that was enough for one day. Twitchell had told him another transaction was scheduled for the following day, so he planned to be waiting tomorrow atop the cliff face overlooking Burro Canyon. He would then see where Sorenson went in Burro Canyon and what he did there.

The next day, Miggs watched through his binoculars from the mesa top as Sorenson entered Burro Canyon, climbed the talus, and disappeared behind a large slab of fallen cap rock. An hour later, he reappeared, descended the talus, and retraced his steps out of the canyon. Miggs took photographs of everything.

He was sure then that he had all he needed for a complete report. He would spend the following day preparing it on his laptop. He would deliver it to Twitchell the day after that and collect his $10,000.

Miggs fumed as he replayed in his mind what had happened then. After he had spent an entire day preparing his report, he'd learned yesterday morning from a newspaper account that Twitchell had been arrested by the FBI and placed in jail. Miggs had done all that work and now he wouldn't be able to collect his fee.

He'd decided then to track down Sorenson's truck and remove the cash from the toolbox, assuming it was still in there. Which he did. He hadn't planned on having to kill Sorenson. The man was just in the wrong place at the wrong time. But he didn't mind killing him. He wasn't the first. In fact, shooting Sorenson had put him on kind of a high. He hadn't killed anyone in a long time. He remembered four years ago when he'd decided to go legit and begin a career as an operative working for detective agencies and law firms. He was pushing forty then and had no desire to spend any more time in the slammer. Before that he'd done hard time in Huntsville for armed robbery and aggravated manslaughter. Those were the crimes the cops knew about. There were several bodies buried in various places in the Painted Desert that they didn't know about. In the old days, contract killing had come easy to him. He'd even found it enjoyable. There had never been any pangs of conscience. He didn't know why or question why—he just accepted that about himself.

This morning, he'd driven his pickup to a remote point on Polar Mesa, found the head of Burro Canyon, and hiked down to the cave. This route kept him far away from the Thompson Canyon Trail and the head of Cottonwood Canyon, which he figured would be crawling with law enforcement people.

He smiled as he thought about everything. In the end, it had all worked out quite well. He was glad his extreme anger over Twitchell's capture had faded. He'd been working on suppressing his violent temper like the prison shrink had taught him, but sometimes it just erupted uncontrollably. Today, though, he felt content. In Sorenson's toolbox, he'd found much more than the ten thousand dollars he'd have gotten from Twitchell. But now he had to figure out what, if anything, he should do about the artifacts in the cave. No doubt they were worth a lot of money, probably big money. Otherwise Twitchell would never have had an interest in them. But what if the police investigation of Sorenson's killing led the cops to the cave? That was a distinct possibility. He decided the best course of action would be to disappear and return in six months to see if the artifacts were still in the cave. And get out of the area right now. That would definitely be the smart thing to do.

His musings were interrupted by a faint thud from outside the cave. It sounded like the closing of a vehicle door. He got up, moved to the entrance, and peered outside. There, down near the mouth of the canyon, was a Sheriff's Department vehicle. And standing next to it was a deputy sheriff. He appeared to be studying a piece of paper.

Miggs withdrew from the entrance and retreated back into the cave. He turned off the lantern and waited in the darkness. Maybe the deputy would finish whatever he was doing and leave. But what if he didn't leave? What if somehow he found the opening to the cave? No problem. He decided he would simply kill the deputy, hike back to Polar Mesa, and split. There was no way he would risk going back to prison. No way.

Miggs moved to a place just inside the cave's entrance. He pulled out his revolver, crouched, and waited.

25

HAVING REREAD LIAM'S letter, Rivera folded it up and stuffed it back into his shirt pocket. He proceeded about one hundred yards into Burro Canyon, passing the place where he'd found the shell casing and the sherd. He stopped and looked left and right, considering which cliff face might hold Josh's cave. Liam's letter didn't specify that detail. Sheer red rock walls rose five hundred feet on either side of the canyon. At the base of these walls, on both sides, were piles of red rock and pink cap rock that had fallen and formed talus slopes. The slopes rose from the canyon floor about one hundred feet up to the cliff faces. A narrow bench had formed at the top of the talus. He scanned the benches, both left and right, looking for a large slab leaning against the canyon wall, one that might possibly conceal an opening to a cave. There were many such slabs on each side, but one in particular on the right side caught his eye. It was leaning against a section of wall that was more whitish-colored than red. It looked like one of those gypsum or limestone intrusions from the Lower Paradox formation that had been squeezed up eons ago into the red sandstone. Rivera recalled from a geology class he'd taken in college that this was a phenomenon not uncommon in the Dolores River Valley. He remembered that this type of rock was more conducive to cave formation, as water slowly dissolved the minerals leaving voids. He decided to check behind that slab first.

He climbed up the talus toward the top, stepping from rock to rock, watching intently where he placed each footstep. Just as he reached the top, he looked up and saw a man emerging from an opening behind the slab. He was a middle-aged man with a hardened face, wearing a tan shirt and jeans. He was holding a snub-nose revolver which was pointed at Rivera.

"Don't!" shouted Rivera as his right hand jerked down reaching for his own piece. The sudden movement caused the rock under his back foot to dislodge, sending Rivera tumbling backwards. He landed painfully on his back, his head downslope and his feet upslope. Worst of all, the fall had badly sprained his right wrist. His right hand and his still-holstered weapon were pinned under the full weight of his body. He was in great pain and was staring uphill at a man with a gun. He wriggled to free his arm but couldn't.

The man was calm and smiling. He extended his arm and pointed the gun down at the defenseless deputy. "So long, cop."

Thoughts of Rivera's family back in Las Cruces raced through his mind. His eyes locked onto the man's eyes and his body stiffened as he braced himself for the inevitable. The gunshot was a loud crack followed by an endless series of reverberations from the canyon walls. As Rivera listened to the fading echoes, he realized the only pain he felt was from the fall. Then he saw the shooter, with a confused look on his face, drop to his knees and fall over on his side. His revolver clattered down the talus.

Rivera rolled over on his left side, managed to get his feet downslope from his head, and struggled to a standing position. The pain in his right arm was extreme and his shoulders, back, and elbows throbbed. Glancing around, he saw Paul Williamson in the distance. He was standing next to his truck at the mouth of Burro Canyon, rifle in hand, looking up at him.

"I had to do it. It looked like he was going to shoot you," shouted Williamson as he trotted over to the base of the talus and climbed up to Rivera.

"Thanks, Mr. Williamson. If you hadn't have shown up when you did, I'd be a dead cop. You saved my life."

"Who is that guy?" said Williamson.

"We'll find out soon enough," said Rivera, gingerly supporting his right arm with his left hand. He knelt down and felt for a pulse. "He's dead." Rivera extracted the man's wallet from the rear pocket of his jeans, wincing as he did from the pain in his arm. "His name is Dexter Miggs. Never heard of him."

"I've never heard of him either. And he doesn't look familiar." Williamson turned away from the dead man, a look of anguish on his face. "I've never shot anyone before."

Rivera felt a bit dizzy and reached out to the cliff face to steady himself. He looked at Williamson. "Would you call back to Moab for me and request that the MedEvac helicopter fly in here and pick up this guy's body? Also tell them to send me some backup."

"Okay. I've got a radio in my truck," said Williamson. "I don't think a chopper can safely drop down in here. The canyon's too narrow and the winds in here can be tricky. There's a flat area about a quarter-mile down Cottonwood Canyon where the canyon floor widens out. They can land there. I'll stay in radio contact and drive the medics back here after they touch down."

"OK. Thanks." Rivera watched Williamson return to his truck, turn it around, and head back down Cottonwood Canyon.

Rivera was suddenly trembling, realizing how close he'd come to death. And his body hurt all over. He moved to a shady spot and sat down, gently leaning his left shoulder against the cliff face for support. After several minutes, the residual fear passed and only the physical pain remained. His thoughts turned to the cave. He wanted to enter it and see what was in there. But he decided to wait outside until the others arrived.

Forty minutes later, Paul Williamson's pickup truck came bouncing into view and stopped. Four doors opened and four men jumped out: Williamson, two paramedics and L.D. Mincey, a Grand County deputy sheriff, sent as Rivera's requested backup. The paramedics retrieved their stretcher and medical cases from the bed of the pickup, trotted over to the base of the talus and climbed up. Mincey, near retirement and overweight, approached at a walk, squinting as he looked up at Rivera.

The paramedics checked Miggs's body, verified he was dead, and turned their attention to Rivera's arm, immobilizing it with a temporary splint. They also treated the cuts on his back and elbows and expressed particular concern about a couple of the deeper gashes. "These could be serious," said the senior paramedic. "You need to get to the hospital and have the doctor check them. They could easily get infected. And that wrist sprain could be a fracture. Needs X-rays. We'd better take you back with us in the chopper."

The paramedics placed Miggs's body on the stretcher, secured it with straps and carried it down the rocky slope and across the canyon floor to the pickup. They tied it down in the bed of the truck and then hoisted themselves into the back seat of the extended-cab vehicle. Rivera gave instructions to Mincey to find and retrieve Miggs's pistol from the talus, bag it as evidence, and then stay the night and guard the cave. No one was to enter.

"But before I leave, I'm going inside the cave for a minute to see what it looks like."

"What's in there?" asked Mincey.

"Come in with me and take a look."

Mincey considered the narrow entrance to the cave and shook his head. "There's no way I could fit through there."

Rivera squeezed himself through the opening, holding his splinted right arm with his left hand, and taking care not to aggravate his injuries. Inside, he reached for the flashlight attached to his belt, turned it on, and scanned the interior of the cave. He could hardly believe his eyes. He'd never before seen such a display of Indian artifacts, not even in a museum. The beam of light passed over large pots on the floor and smaller pots and figurines set on various flat surfaces higher up. The beam also illuminated a skeleton in ragged clothes in the back of the cave. Rivera wanted to make a closer inspection but his arm starting throbbing again. He decided it was time to leave. Tomorrow he would return and perform a thorough investigation. And now he had another mystery to solve. Whose skeleton was that?

He exited the cave and spoke to Mincey. "The cave's full of Indian artifacts. Pots and bowls and so forth. Probably very valuable. There's also a human skeleton in there. Make sure no one enters the cave until I return tomorrow. I'll radio the sheriff from the chopper and fill him in on what happened here."

"Don't worry, Manny. I'll take care of things. I brought a couple of blankets and enough food to last me until tomorrow."

"Thanks, L.D."

Rivera gingerly worked his way down the talus and walked toward Williamson's tan extended-cab pickup truck. Williamson, wearing a black cowboy hat, was standing outside the vehicle waiting for him. Suddenly another piece of the puzzle clicked into place. Rivera remembered what the letterboxer from Northern Arizona University had told him. He'd seen a large man wearing a dark cowboy hat carrying a smaller man to a light-colored pickup truck with four doors. Instantly he knew who had moved Montoya's body. But he didn't yet know why.

As he approached Williamson, Rivera said, "Thanks again for saving my life, Mr. Williamson." He paused. He looked at the truck and back at Williamson. "I'll be back here tomorrow to talk to you. And you've got a lot of explaining to do."

Williamson stood silently for a moment, giving Rivera a long measured look. Then he blinked and his gaze dropped to the ground. He shook his head. "It was a stupid thing to do but I had a good reason. I'll be at the ranch house tomorrow waiting for you."

26

WHEN HE AWOKE the next morning, Rivera found himself in a private room in the Allen Memorial Hospital in Moab. His arm was in a permanent cast, still hurting, but the pain wasn't as sharp as it had been last night. The cuts and bruises he'd received from the fall stung a little less. Now, getting out of the hospital and returning to work was his top priority.

He'd arrived by helicopter late yesterday and after the doctors had examined him, he was informed that not only was his wrist sprained but he also had a fractured forearm. On top of that, they wanted to watch him for signs of concussion and give him a round of IV antibiotics to guard against infections in the puncture wounds he'd suffered in the fall. The doctors said he should remain in the hospital overnight. It was a slow night in the emergency room so he received a lot of attention from the medical staff. The one thing he remembered most was the nurse who assisted the doctors in his treatment—an attractive Hispanic lady he'd never seen before.

His first visitor was Sheriff Bradshaw who arrived promptly at 9:00 A.M., just as Rivera was swallowing the analgesic and muscle relaxants the medication nurse had brought him. Bradshaw had visited the previous night to check on his deputy and get an overview of what had happened. He'd deferred an in-depth debriefing until morning so Rivera could get some rest. But now he wanted to know everything. Rivera detailed his encounter with Miggs, Williamson's timely appearance at the scene, and the arrival of the paramedics and Deputy Mincey by MedEvac helicopter. He told the sheriff about the cave, the artifacts it contained, and the skeleton. He said he planned to return to the cave today with the Medical Examiner to investigate the skeleton. They needed to identify it and determine the cause of death. Before he departed, the sheriff smiled and congratulated Rivera on a job well done.

His next visitors were Emmett Mitchell and Adam Dunne. They arrived together. After listening to the whole story, they asked a lot of questions and generally poked fun at him for letting Miggs get the drop on him. Good natured ribbing about quick-draw Rivera, the cop with his shooting hand in a cast, and so forth. Rivera appreciated their visit and enjoyed the camaraderie. It lifted his spirits. But his thoughts always came back to the skeleton in the back of the cave.

After they departed, he was eager to leave the hospital, return to Burro Canyon, and get started on the rest of the investigation. He swung his legs out of bed and stood up, grimacing from the pain in his back and right shoulder. No doubt about it—he was going to be stiff and sore for a few weeks. He washed his face, brushed his teeth as best he could with his left hand, and got dressed. That done, he sat down on the edge of the bed and picked up the phone. He dialed Dr. Pudge Devlin's number using one of the fingers of his right hand which remained exposed outside of the cast. He told the Medical Examiner about what he'd found in the cave and asked if they could meet at the front gate of the Rutherford Ranch around 3:00 P.M. Devlin said he would be there.

Rivera called the nurses station to find out how soon he could be discharged. A pleasant voice told him the doctor would visit his room in about an hour and let him know. A short time later, the pretty nurse he remembered from the night before entered the room.

"How are you feeling," she asked.

"Much better this morning, thanks," Rivera said. He found himself instantly attracted to her. He glanced furtively at her left hand and noted she wasn't wearing a wedding ring.

She smiled at him. She was about five-foot six with dark hair and green eyes. Even in her green scrubs, he could see she was slim and shapely. She had the athletic look of someone who enjoyed outdoor activities. He guessed her age to be about 25.

"My name is Vivian Ramos," she said, still smiling.

"Hi, I'm Manny Rivera. Slightly busted up but otherwise intact." She laughed. "It's a pleasure to meet you," he said. "I haven't seen you before. Have you lived in Moab very long?

"Not long at all. I moved here a month ago from Taos. There was an opening for a nurse at the hospital so I applied and was accepted. I love this area. My aunt has lived in Moab for twenty years so I've visited often. I'd always hoped for a chance to live here. The job opening finally made it possible."

They chatted for about fifteen minutes, getting to know one another. Rivera was surprised at how easy it was to talk to her. It was small talk but they were having fun, enjoying each other's company. They even joked about the challenges of being Hispanic in a mostly Anglo community.

"Be warned," laughed Rivera. "You can't get a decent enchilada in this town. There are four Mexican restaurants here and not one of them makes enchiladas the way I like them. My family lives in Las Cruces. My grandmother makes world-class enchiladas so I go back there as often as I can just to eat a plateful. And, of course, I miss the people down there." He realized he was rambling on, but he enjoyed talking to this lady. She asked him what he was doing that led to his injuries, and he summarized the events of the past week for her. She seemed impressed. He liked that. Then she asked him about the letterboxing part of the story. She said she wasn't familiar with it but it sounded like a great idea. Rivera told her about the four students who introduced him to letterboxing and how much fun they'd been having. He said he wanted to spend more time in the future experiencing the backcountry like those young people had been doing.

His story was interrupted by the buzzing sound of Vivian's hospital pager. She looked at it and said, "I've got to go. I enjoyed talking with you. Take care." Then she was gone.

Just after she left, the doctor walked in. "How are you feeling, Manny?"

"I'm fine, Doctor. Sore muscles and the arm aches. But the pills help a lot. I've got to get back to work. How soon can I check out of here?"

The doctor looked at Rivera's chart, studied it briefly. Then he looked at Rivera. "Do you feel light-headed at all?" Rivera answered in the negative. The doctor paused, studying his patient's face for a moment. "Okay, Manny, you're good to go," he said finally. "But be careful with that arm. That cast is strong, but please, no more falling on rocks."

As Rivera walked down the hospital corridor toward the exit, he glanced up and down each intersecting hallway, hoping for one last look at Vivian. But she was nowhere to be seen. He left the hospital, rode back to the Sheriff's Office with a fellow deputy who'd been sent to collect him, and obtained a vehicle.

During the long drive across the mountains to the Rutherford Ranch, a drive which had to be negotiated with one hand, Rivera had a lot of time to think and many things to think about. Having solved the Montoya case, he felt a deep sense of satisfaction. There was probably some luck involved, but Bradshaw's counsel had proved correct. Take one step, evaluate the results, and then take the next step. Make your own luck. And finding Sorenson's killer didn't take long. It was mostly happenstance. But now he had another mystery to solve. Who was the skeleton in the cave? How and when did he or she die? And was there a crime involved? He and Devlin would begin investigating those questions later in the afternoon. Realizing now that he thoroughly enjoyed detective work, Rivera found himself looking forward to solving this next mystery.

His thoughts turned to Sorenson. He had messed up his life, trading an academic life he loved for the lure of wealth. He'd needlessly died ashamed and unfulfilled. Had Sorenson considered all the possibilities before he'd stolen artifacts from private property and killed a man? After he'd found the cave, he could have simply reported it to the university and the ranch owner—then he could have published the details of the cave's contents in an anthropological journal. This would have helped establish him as a serious scholar and a promising PhD candidate. Had Sorenson thought of that?

In an odd way, Rivera had liked Sorenson. Under different circumstances, they might have been friends. He admired the way Sorenson had tracked down the cave just as Sorenson had admired him for finding it. The man's dying words still rang in Rivera's ears, "I feel ashamed." What a sad and disappointing final thought for a man to have. Rivera recalled what his grandfather used to tell him: "The smaller your desire for material things, the larger your happiness." Rivera knew from a comparative philosophy course he'd taken at the university that this was the belief professed by most of the great thinkers since the beginning of history. Why was it so hard for people to understand? If only Sorenson had had the benefit of his grandfather's advice, his life might have turned out differently.

Rivera saw a pair of mourning doves in the road up ahead and hit the brakes, slowing to a crawl. Why did they always wait until the last possible second before flying out of the way? Beautiful and mysterious birds. For some reason, that thought caused Vivian Ramos to appear in his thoughts. Maybe he would see her again around town. He wished he was a little surer of himself with women. He knew he was blessed with good looks and a certain amount of charm, and he was accustomed to getting a lot of attention from the ladies. But he lacked confidence in his ability to judge their character.

He'd had a few brief relationships over the years, but none very serious or satisfying. In each case, for one reason or another, he had ended up disappointed by some character flaw or personality trait that turned him off. He wondered about Vivian. She seemed like a first-class lady. Maybe she would be the one.

Recalling her questions about letterboxing, he was reminded of his own interest in giving it a try. He was serious about making more time for the things that brought him pleasure, and letterboxing was number one on the list.

After the long drive across the mountains, Rivera reached the head of John Brown Canyon. He stopped the vehicle and considered the gravel road ahead, a long series of sharp curves with steep drop-offs and no guard rails. Driving it with two hands was difficult enough, but having the use of only one hand would make it even more challenging. He proceeded slowly.

After he'd negotiated the winding descent and driven through Gateway, his thoughts turned to his unfinished business with Paul Williamson. There were a lot of unanswered questions. Williamson had moved Montoya's body off the ranch and up to the Kokopelli Trail. He'd admitted as much. But why? Rivera owed his life to Williamson, but tampering with crime-scene evidence and obstructing a murder investigation were felonies. He would get to the bottom of it today.

But first he would meet Devlin and return to the cave. The doctor was waiting for him at the entrance to the Rutherford Ranch. Rivera gave him a "follow me" gesture and the two vehicles entered the ranch, turned west about a half-mile before the ranch house, and crossed the pastures. At the entrance to the canyon, Rivera stopped and considered the rocky road ahead. He exited his vehicle, and walked back to Devlin's truck. "Maybe you should leave your truck behind and drive my vehicle, Doc. I don't think I could hang on to the steering wheel on this road without damaging my arm." Devlin grabbed his medical bag and followed Rivera back to his unit, sliding in behind the steering wheel.

"I've always wanted to drive one of these things," he said. "How do I turn on the siren?"

Rivera laughed. He always enjoyed Devlin's company. The two men slowly made their way up Cottonwood Canyon. They arrived at Burro Canyon, parked next to Rivera's original vehicle, and ascended the talus toward the cave. Deputy Mincey, sitting in a shady spot with his back against the canyon wall, was sound asleep.

"I don't get paid enough to do this climbing," protested Devlin. "I'm gonna put in for hazardous duty pay."

"Just fill out the form in triplicate, Doc. Send it directly to me," said Rivera, smiling.

The banter woke Mincey up. "What took you guys so long? My butt is real sore from sitting on this rock." He slowly unfolded his body and stood up.

"Sorry about that, L.D. And thanks for looking after things. Deputy Sanders will be here in about three hours to relieve you. You can head back to Moab as soon as he arrives."

"Okay, Manny," said Mincey, stretching like a man who was stiff all over. "I'll be glad when my retirement rolls around in five months. Then it'll be nothing but fishing for me."

"Then you'll be sitting on a rock holding a fishing pole instead of just sitting on a rock," said Rivera, smiling.

Mincey chuckled. "When I go fishing, I'll bring a soft chair. And while you guys are in the cave, I'm going to go down and get in the vehicle. I need something soft to sit on right now." He descended the talus.

"In here," said Rivera to Devlin, pointing to the opening behind the sandstone slab.

"You've got to be kidding," said a hesitant Devlin. "I can't fit through there."

"Sure you can, Doc. Just suck it in. I'll go in first and pull you through," said Rivera, grinning and enjoying the situation. Rivera squeezed inside, carrying two propane lanterns in his good hand. Then it was Devlin's turn. He sized up the opening, approached it reluctantly and began a process of careful maneuvering and squirming. More than once, he had to reach down with both hands, grasp his belly, hoist it up and advance it forward. After an extended period of grunting accompanied by hysterical laughter, both men were inside the cave, Devlin smiling and breathing hard from the ordeal.

"I'm glad that's over."

"It's not over yet, Doc. You still have to get out," said Rivera, still grinning.

After the lanterns were ignited, the two men stood there without a word, looking around. The air in the cave was cool and stale, the walls a light gray color. Large pots were resting on the floor of the cave and smaller pots and figurines sat in the walls wherever nature had provided a flat spot. Each artifact had been placed on a bed of straw for protection, and it was evident from the empty straw beds that a large number of items had been removed from the cave.

Rivera began the process of taking inventory and photographing the artifacts while Devlin knelt in front of the skeleton and studied it. It was lying on its back draped in rags that were once clothing. Faded leather boots were still in place on the feet. The dry air in the cave had partially mummified the corpse. There was still some dried skin and yellow hair on the skull. A faded, dusty cowboy hat rested against the wall, covered with spider webs.

Devlin spoke. "The corpse looks like it's been dead for a long time. Probably over fifty years. I'll have to get it back to the lab and run some tests to get a better estimate of the year of death. Right now I'd say it was a male who died when he was between twenty and forty years of age. No obvious signs of foul play."

Rivera came over and knelt down next to Devlin to get a closer look. After taking photographs, he checked the pockets of the tattered jeans and removed an old leather wallet, a few coins, and a faded blue and white handkerchief. As he opened the wallet, the leather cracked and emitted a puff of dust. Behind a yellowing plastic window was a black-and-white picture of a young woman. An identification card in the wallet revealed the name of the owner: Liam Scott.

"Well, I'll be damned," said Rivera. "This is the fellow who wrote all those letters. Becky's boyfriend." He put the wallet and its contents into an evidence bag. Then he noticed something protruding from the shirt pocket. He reached over and slid it out, the cloth of the pocket crumbling as he did. It was an old letter, the envelope's paper now a light brown color. The ink had faded but the handwriting was still readable. The address on the envelope was Rebecca Ann Cross, 16 Summerville Lane, Colorado Springs 6, Colorado. Time had decomposed the glue on the envelope's flap so it was easily opened. The envelope contained a letter and what appeared to be a silver locket. Rather than examine them here in the cave, Rivera placed the envelope and its contents into a second evidence bag. It would be better to study them back at the office.

Sometime later, after completing their work, the two men left the cave, descended the talus, and said goodbye to Mincey. They walked toward Rivera's vehicle.

"I'll have the remains moved to the morgue in the morning and perform an examination to determine cause of death," said Devlin.

"Okay, Doc. Thanks."

They drove back down Cottonwood Canyon to Devlin's vehicle where Devlin got out and said goodbye. The two vehicles then caravaned across the west pasture until they arrived at the main ranch road. Here, Devlin turned right and headed back to Moab via Gateway, and Rivera turned left and headed toward the ranch headquarters. As Rivera drove up to the house, he could see old Mr. Rutherford sitting as usual in his rocking chair on the porch. Paul Williamson appeared at the door and invited Rivera to come inside.

"We need to talk," said Rivera.

"Sarah's in Moab at the children's home," said Williamson. "So we have the place to ourselves." They entered the living room and sat down in overstuffed chairs facing each other. Williamson took a deep breath and let it out. "I'll tell you the whole story," he said. "And it's a long one."

Two hours later, Rivera left the ranch house, his brain aching. Williamson's explanation for having moved Montoya's body had been extraordinary. Rivera slowly drove across the mountain roads in the dark of night, handicapped by the cast on his right arm but grateful for an almost-full moon which helped illuminate the route. As he reviewed and analyzed everything Williamson had told him, he was left with a king-sized ethical dilemma. He had no idea what to do. He decided he needed to talk to someone. Get some advice. It would have to be someone outside of law enforcement. Someone with a lot more wisdom than he had. He thought of his grandfather.

27

AT HOME THAT evening, Rivera picked up the telephone and called his grandparents in Las Cruces. For a long time before he dialed their number, he'd sat in his dimly-lit living room thinking about the difficult decision he would have to make in the morning. He was looking forward to explaining the Williamson situation to his grandfather and seeking the benefit of his wisdom. He would tell him the whole story from the beginning, leaving out the part where Miggs had almost killed him. And then he would ask for his grandfather's advice. He respected the wisdom of the older man more than anyone else he knew. His grandfather had a knack for reducing what seemed to be a complex problem down to its essence.

As he listened to the phone ringing, he was grateful to be part of his large extended family. His grandmother answered.

"Abuelita, it's Manny."

"Manny! It's so wonderful to hear from you. How are you?" The joy he heard in her voice made him smile.

They spoke at length, even though he was anxious to talk with his grandfather. He told her he was doing fine in Moab and missed them both very much. She told him about family and friends in Las Cruces, who was doing what, who said what. Unspoken by his grandmother was her wish, and the wish of the entire family, that he return for good someday. She was too loving and respectful to reiterate what she'd gently told him years ago, that Las Cruces was his home and he shouldn't stray so far from family.

"Abuelita, I'll be home soon for a visit."

"Oh, Manny, we'll be so happy to see you. I'll make you some enchiladas, just the way you like them."

They talked a while longer and then he asked to speak with his grandfather. After some small talk, Rivera got to the point.

"I need some advice, Grandfather. I have a long story I'd like to tell you, and then, at the end, I'd like to ask you a question. Do you have time to listen to a long story?"

"I always have time for you, Manny."

And so Rivera began, starting at the beginning. He talked about the mountain bikers finding Montoya's body, the autopsy during which a potsherd stuck into the skin was discovered, and about the letterboxers and what one of them had seen in Burro Canyon. He told of his subsequent visit to that canyon and the shell casing and second potsherd he found there. He went on to describe his visit to the university, the discovery of the reconstructed pot in the ceramics lab, and its two missing pieces. He spoke about his search of Sorenson's office, the discovery of the diaries, the visit to the Vance residence in Vernal, the contents of Liam's letters which led to the discovery of the cave, and finally, the killing of Sorenson by Miggs. Carefully avoiding any mention of his close brush with death and his visit to the hospital, he concluded by saying that Miggs was shot and killed yesterday at the cave by Paul Williamson, the Rutherford Ranch foreman, thereby saving another man's life.

He described his conversation with Sorenson as he was dying, and explained how it was he knew Williamson was the one who had moved Montoya's body off the ranch to BLM land.

"Are you following all this, Grandfather?"

"Yes I am, Manny. Take your time."

Rivera described his visit to the Rutherford Ranch earlier in the day and his direct question to Williamson: "Why did you move Jesse Montoya's body from Burro Canyon all the way up to the Kokopelli Trail?"

Williamson's response had been long and detailed: "First of all, Sarah knows nothing about my moving the body. The reason I moved it goes back to something that happened a long time ago. When Sarah first got involved as a volunteer at the children's home, the place was barely getting along. It was under-financed, under-managed, and under-appreciated in the community. It housed seven children ranging from three to nine years of age. The facilities consisted of an old house on four acres of land. The house was badly in need of repair. The vegetable garden was full of weeds and the kids were using a decrepit old work shed in the back as their play area. The facilities were pathetic but the volunteer staff made up for it with hard work and love. The state of Utah was very appreciative of the volunteers, but insisted the children's home had to meet the State's codes and standards. Of course, it didn't. Not even close. So Sarah began to take a more active role in the management of the place. She and I were never able to have children, so the kids at the home filled a void for her.

"As Sarah got more involved, I did too. I spent my free time repairing plumbing, cracked windows, electrical wiring that didn't meet code, and so forth. In those years, the size of the herd was small due to chronically low beef prices, so Mr. Rutherford allowed me to spend a lot of time helping out at the home. Then Mr. Rutherford himself began to take an interest in the home. Sarah's involvement and enthusiasm had rubbed off on him, too.

"There's another part of this history that's important. Mr. Rutherford had no kin except for one son who'd gone bad. He was on death row in Texas for committing multiple murders. A real bad character.

For Mr. Rutherford, who had always led an exemplary life, this had been a cruel blow. One day, he decided to change his will, leaving everything in trust to the children's home with Sarah and me as trustees. He realized that bequeathing the ranch to his son made no sense. Wouldn't do anybody any good. He told us that after he passed away, he wanted Sarah and me to continue operating the ranch, with the profits going to the children's home. And, of course, we would be able to continue living the life we love.

"Then, before he could change his will, Mr. Rutherford died."

At this point in the story, Rivera explained to his grandfather about the old man sitting on the porch in his rocking chair, staring out toward the Dolores River each day, and never speaking to anyone. He said the Williamson's had simply let him and everyone else assume the old man was Mr. Rutherford. Then he continued telling the story as Williamson had related it:

"Mr. Rutherford was an elderly man. One morning about six years ago we found him dead in his bed. Died in his sleep during the night. We buried him in a remote part of the ranch in a beautiful grove of cottonwood trees. I put a wrought iron fence around the grave to keep the cattle out. Sarah and I placed a cross at the gravesite but there's no marker showing who's buried there. We decided not to report Mr. Rutherford's death because that was the only way we could respect his wishes for supporting the children's home. Otherwise the ranch would go to his son who would have absolutely no use for it. It would just end up being the property of the lawyers and the state. And of course, we had our own selfish reasons — we loved our life here on the ranch. Leaving all this to a low-life on death row and sacrificing the children's home in the process made no sense to us. We knew what we were doing was illegal, but it seemed to serve a greater good."

Rivera said, "At this point, Grandfather, I advised Mr. Williamson he was admitting to a crime, probably three or four crimes, and I needed to read him his rights. He said there was no need, he knew his rights. So I let him continue."

"We felt we were doing the right thing," he said, "and I hope you'll see it that way too. Sarah had an uncle who was old and declining mentally and physically. We were the only family he had, so we brought him here to take care of him. That's the man you've seen sitting on the porch in the rocking chair. At the time he arrived, there were no ranch hands working here. Sarah and I did all the work. As I said, the cattle market was real soft back then, so cash from the ranch operations was insufficient to pay for additional help. Every day was a struggle but we were happy. Then one day an employee of the electric company drove onto the ranch to make some measurements on a power line that passes through here. He greeted us, then turned to Sarah's uncle and said "Good morning, Mr. Rutherford." We didn't correct him. We just let him believe the man on the porch was Mr. Rutherford. And after that, we did the same thing with everyone else who visited the ranch. The few friends that Mr. Rutherford had had were long since deceased. No one who would recognize him came around anymore.

"Eventually the price of beef went up and the rains were more kind to the pastures, so we were able to rebuild the herd. We hired a few hands and of course, we let them believe the old man was Mr. Rutherford. In recent years the ranch has become profitable. Sarah still keeps the books and pays the bills, just as she did when Mr. Rutherford was alive. He had authorized her to sign his name to the checks and she still does.

"After we pay the ranch expenses and our own living expenses, the rest goes to the children's home. In the last few years, we've built two new buildings on the grounds. One is a modern dormitory and the other is a house with a day room, an office, an entertainment area, and three classrooms. The children's home is now certified by the state and supports thirty-six kids. Sarah is the Board Chairwoman and has been successful in getting the support of the City and County Councils. It's become a model home, but it still exists on a hand-to-mouth basis. There are now several paid employees, including a director, but a lot of volunteer help is still needed from people in the community. There's very little money in the home's bank account. The proceeds from the ranch are substantial, but can only support the home's day-to-day operations. Contributions from the people of Moab help a great deal, but without the money from the ranch operations, the children's home would go broke in a month.

"I moved Montoya's body because I didn't want an investigation of the ranch itself. I had no idea why Montoya had been shot, but I did know he was a doper. Maybe only a user, but maybe worse—I wasn't sure. When I found him dead in Burro Canyon, I figured he was probably dealing and got cross-ways with the wrong people. I also figured the ranch would be investigated to see if we were involved in the drug trade, and then everything we'd done about concealing Mr. Rutherford's death would come out. Sarah would be crushed, the children's home would cease to exist, and all our efforts would have been for nothing. I couldn't take that chance."

After Rivera related all this to his grandfather, he added, "I've taken an oath to uphold the law." Then he waited. After a brief silence, his grandfather spoke.

"Manny, the whole point of laws and law enforcement is to keep the community a civilized place to live. A place where people can be born, lead productive lives, raise families and have a chance at peace and happiness. The lawmakers do the best they can making the laws, but they can't foresee every possible set of circumstances. Justice is more important than the letter of the law. In this case you have to make the call. How is justice best served here? You're obligated to enforce the law. You took an oath. But sometimes justice and the law are on different sides."

As Rivera placed the telephone back into its cradle, he felt a heavy burden. He knew he would have to make an important decision before finalizing his report tomorrow. He unwrapped the now lukewarm hamburger he'd bought earlier, looked at it, and thought again about his grandmother's enchiladas.

28

THE FOLLOWING DAY, Manny Rivera was back in his office, trying to wrap things up. It was late afternoon and he was tired. And having to do everything with his left hand wasn't helping. Eating and getting dressed were especially difficult and made him feel clumsy. He was glad no one had seen him trying to brush his teeth or comb his hair. But, all in all, it had been a rewarding day. Matters surrounding the Montoya murder had fallen into place. The jigsaw puzzle was now complete. He was finishing his long and detailed report. Because of the cast on his arm, he had to dictate it into a machine rather than type it. The sheriff's secretary had said she would type the report for him as soon as he finished it. That left Rivera to master the art of dictating. Talking into the machine made him feel self-conscious, but he'd been able to accomplish it and was now nearing the end of the report.

The day had begun with visits and calls from the press. Word had spread quickly throughout Moab about the deaths of Sorenson and Miggs. From the time Montoya's body was found one week ago, the press had referred to his murderer as the *Canyon Killer*, a term which certainly hadn't enhanced the prospects of backcountry tourism. The second killing had caused even greater consternation. But now that both cases had been resolved, the canyons were proclaimed to once again be safe for hiking. There had been visits by reporters from the *Times-Independent* and the *Salt Lake Tribune* and even telephone calls from the Associated Press and CNN. The highlight of the morning was a call from an adventure magazine wanting to do a feature article on the whole story. Sheriff Bradshaw handled the interviews himself, and was always quick to point out that both cases had been broken by the superb detective work of Deputy Sheriff Manny Rivera. Bradshaw had been generous with sincere praise and admiration, and Rivera's co-workers had been treating him like a hero all day. All the attention revived in Rivera the hope that all was forgotten about how he'd bungled the marijuana patch stakeout last month.

There had also been congratulatory telephone calls from city and county officials and representatives of the Moab area tourism community. The entire county was showing its appreciation and relief that the matter had been resolved.

By late morning, Miggs's pickup truck had been recovered from where it was parked on Polar Mesa. It was brought to the Sheriff's office where a search was conducted. The glove compartment yielded paper bags filled with cash, and Sorenson's fingerprints were found on several of the one hundred dollar bills. The truck also contained a report detailing the surveillance of Frank Sorenson for the past several days. The report listed Donald Twitchell of Farmington, New Mexico as the client.

Sorenson's artifact list was identical to the one found by the FBI in the back room of Twitchell's Indian Artifacts store. The accompanying photographs in Twitchell's office were identical to pots still in the cave. The linkage between Sorenson, Twitchell, and Miggs had been firmly established.

The FBI and the sheriff agreed that the pots in the cave properly belonged to the Rutherford Ranch. The cash recovered from the truck and the funds in Sorenson's three bank accounts were likewise the property of Mr. Rutherford. Any funds the FBI could recover from Twitchell's previous sales of Rutherford property would be returned. The view was that Sorenson had simply stolen private property. So the Sorenson end of the case became the responsibility of the Grand County Sheriff's Office while the Twitchell end, a federal offense involving violation of the Antiquities Act, would be prosecuted by the FBI.

And so, the Montoya and Sorenson mysteries had been solved and Rivera had completed his report. It detailed the chronology of events from the discovery of Montoya's body up to the present. Rivera leaned back in his chair, satisfied that the report was complete in every detail. Every detail except one. There was no mention of Paul Williamson's having moved Montoya's body. Let everyone believe Sorenson had moved the body away from the cave in an effort to protect its location. The kids in the Children's Home had a stake in this too. As his grandfather had said, enforcing the law and serving justice are not always the same thing. Rivera turned off the recording machine and gave the tape to the sheriff's secretary.

Later in the afternoon, Rivera received a phone call from Paul Williamson.

"I just wanted you to know that next week, Sarah will announce that, thanks to certain benefactors, a pledge of six hundred thousand dollars has been made to set up an endowment for the Moab Home for Needy Children."

Rivera smiled. "That's great news. Who are the benefactors?"

"It's their desire to remain anonymous. But I understand they're selling a valuable collection of Indian artifacts to finance the pledge."

After that, Dr. Pudge Devlin had visited Rivera and reported the results of the autopsy he'd performed on Liam's remains. As best Devlin could determine, Liam had fallen and cracked his head on a rock. There was a fracture on the back of the skull but no definitive sign of foul play. And, of course, if foul play had been involved, the treasures in the cave would likely have been removed by the perpetrator. So Liam's death was declared accidental.

After Devlin departed, Rivera sat at his desk, thinking about Liam. He opened the envelope he'd removed from Liam's shirt pocket and removed the locket and the letter. He released the catch on the locket and saw the two pictures it contained: a young Becky and a young Liam. Then he unfolded the letter and reread it:

September 3, 1938

Dearest Becky,

I'm sorry my last letter was so short. Well, I've thought a lot about what to do with these pots. I'm going to keep a few for us and sell the rest to get enough cash so we can buy our own ranch and start our life together. The problem I've been mulling over is how to get the pots out of the cave without being seen by ranch hands that might be working in the canyon. I also have to be sure that no one in town gets wise to my new source of wealth and tries to follow me to the cave. So I've decided that I'll bring back two or three pots each trip wrapped in beaver skins as though I'd been trapping in the mountains. I have a friend in Monticello who travels a lot and who I can trust to sell them to collectors for me.

I had the enclosed silver locket made for you. I hope you like it. It snaps open and on the inside is your picture on one side and mine on the other. I cut them out of one of the pictures we had taken in the photo booth that day we met at the County Fair. The back is engraved, "I love you."

Now I'm a man of means thanks to Josh. So if it's OK with you, I'd like to come to Colorado Springs around the end of September so we can get married. Can you arrange for a preacher? My heart is bursting with joy. I love you so much.

All my love always,
Liam

Rivera swallowed as he placed the locket and letter back into the envelope. He felt a deep sadness that Liam and Becky were never able to finish their love story.

29

RIVERA SLOWLY PULLED his Grand County Sheriff's Department vehicle up to the curb in front of the Cenizo Home for the Elderly. It was early afternoon. The dark clouds gathering overhead meant rain would be arriving soon. A chill was in the air.

The home was a sprawling grayish-white colonial structure with a wooden veranda spanning the front of the building. Rivera guessed it was built in the early 1900s. It was set back from the road on about six acres of land and was surrounded by large elm and cotton-wood trees. The building was beyond its prime. The paint was peeling in many places. The asphalt circular drive was broken along the edges, its surface an array of patchwork. The lawn was in need of mowing and weeds had begun to assert themselves.

On the veranda was a collection of white wicker chairs, some occupied by grey-haired ladies sitting in small groups. An elderly bald man with thick glasses sat quietly off to one side by himself. Rivera stepped out of his vehicle, took in the scene, and felt a shiver.

Seeing old people living lonely lives had always made him uncomfortable. He wasn't sure exactly why. Perhaps it was because one day he too would be old, sitting in a rocking chair, and trying to find someone interested in hearing the stories of his life. As he ascended the stairs to the veranda, the residents became silent. All eyes followed him as he went through the front doorway and proceeded to the director's office.

Rivera introduced himself to the director, reminded him of their previous telephone conversation, and explained in general terms the nature of his visit. "Is Becky in the building?" he asked.

"Yes, she's in her room. The door is usually open and I'm sure she'll be willing to receive you. But as I told you before, she doesn't speak anymore. Hasn't uttered a word in years. Just stares out the window. Her mind is still sharp so she'll understand everything you say to her." He pointed the way. "She's down that hallway, last door on the left."

Rivera knocked softly on Becky's door which was open. She looked up at him and smiled. She had a kind and intelligent face. Her shoulder-length white hair was neatly combed and she was wearing a light blue dress with a white collar. She was seated in a stuffed chair next to a window which looked out onto the grass and trees.

He entered the room, holding his hat with both hands, his head bowed slightly. He kept eye contact with

Becky and managed a smile. He sat down in a chair across from her. Resting his forearms on his knees, he leaned forward and began in a solemn tone. "Ms. Cross, I'm Deputy Sheriff Manny Rivera from Grand County just south of here. My office is in Moab." He cleared his throat. "I have some news."

Becky's expression was unchanged. She continued smiling, her hazel eyes locked onto his.

"We found Liam. I'm sorry to tell you he's been dead for a long time. His body was discovered in a cave in a remote canyon."

Becky's eyes widened and filled with tears. Her smile melted away and her face became expressionless. Rivera shifted in his chair.

"The Medical Examiner said the likely cause of death was a skull fracture caused by an accidental fall. He died in 1938. We know that because he had a letter addressed to you in his shirt pocket."

Becky drew in a breath and looked at him expectantly.

"I brought the letter with me," he said, reaching into his pocket and handing her Liam's last letter. She reached for it and held it with both hands next to her heart for a moment. Then she picked up her reading glasses from the small round table next to her chair and put them on. She opened the envelope and extracted the letter and the locket. She gazed at the locket, her smile now returning. She tried to open it but her frail hands couldn't manage. Rivera reached over and gently pressed the release. The locket popped open. Becky's smile grew wider, a tear now flowing down her cheek. She looked up at Rivera with appreciation in her eyes.

She began reading the letter, holding it with trembling hands. Rivera, thinking this was the right time to depart, rose from his chair. He quietly left the room, stepped out into the hallway, and began closing the door to give Becky her privacy. Just before the door clicked shut, Rivera heard her murmur, "Oh, Liam. . ."

As he walked down the hallway back to the reception area, he thought to himself that finally, after all these years of waiting and wondering, Becky's obsession with the question of death or abandonment had been answered.

Rivera descended the front steps of the Cenizo Home and walked toward his vehicle. He glanced back at the veranda, his eyes falling on the old man sitting by himself. The man silently stared back at him. Rivera looked away and continued toward his vehicle, knowing he needed to do something about his own life.

He got into his vehicle, picked up his cell phone, and dialed the hospital. He asked to speak to Vivian Ramos.

EPILOGUE

Vernal, Utah
Two Weeks Later

THE SUN CAST dappled shadows across the manicured lawn and white gravestones of the Vernal Memorial Cemetery. Vivian Ramos stood next to Manny Rivera, holding his arm. A cool breeze rustled the cottonwood trees where they were standing and a few more golden leaves drifted to the ground. He looked at her, remembering the first time he had seen her. She was pretty then in her green scrubs, but was stunning now in a straight black dress. He smiled as he remembered their conversation when he called her at the hospital two weeks ago. He'd invited her to go letterboxing with him on her next day off. She'd said yes but had one condition: that afterwards, he let her fix him some homemade enchiladas. They'd been inseparable ever since.

Becky stood on the green grass in front of the freshly turned soil of Liam's gravesite. She was wearing a dark blue dress. The silver heart-shaped locket from Liam hung from a chain around her neck. Kenneth and Jill Vance, standing on either side of Becky, had picked her up at the Cenizo Home for the Elderly and driven her to the cemetery.

A week ago, Becky had purchased two adjacent burial sites with the help of the Vances. Liam's remains had been interred in one of them. A small headstone inscribed with Liam's name, date of birth, and date of death was placed at the head of his grave. The date on Liam's last letter was used for the date of death. The second burial site was reserved for Becky.

The young minister in attendance, a preacher from the Vances' church, had just finished speaking and was closing his bible. He stepped around the gravesite and approached Becky. She reached out and grasped his extended hand. "Thank you so much for the beautiful ceremony," she whispered. Since she'd read Liam's last letter, she'd started talking again.

As the preacher departed, Becky turned to the Vances, Rivera, and Vivian. "Thank you all for coming today," she managed, a tear rolling down her cheek. "Liam and I appreciate it very much."

The group quietly walked from the gravesite to their vehicles which were parked on the pavement nearby. Rivera opened the door of his vehicle, reached in, and extracted a framed photograph. He walked back to Becky and gently placed it in her hands. It was an enhanced enlargement of one of the three photographs from the shoebox. Framed in polished redwood, it showed Liam and Becky smiling, standing in front of her mother's house in Colorado Springs. Becky gazed at the image and smiled, tears again welling in her eyes.

She looked up at him. "Thank you so much for this, Deputy Rivera." She took another long look at the photograph, and then smiled at Rivera. "And thank you for finding Liam for me."

Later that evening, Becky sat alone in her room, looking at the framed photograph that rested in her lap. The radio that had sat silently in her room for years was now filling the room with soft music. She was happy again. The question that had hung heavy in her mind all these years had finally been answered. All doubt was gone. Liam had truly loved her.

Other titles in the Manny Rivera Mystery Series:

February's Files (#2)

Trails of Deception (#3)

MoonShadow Murder (#4)

Deadly Games (#5)

Death Saint (#6)

Author's Website:

www.richcurtinnovels.com

CPSIA information can be obtained
at www.ICGtesting.com
Printed in the USA
FSHW021318170619
59135FS